THE COMPLETE CASES OF SEEKAY

PAUL ERNST

THE COMPLETE CASES OF

SEEKAY™

PAUL ERNST

INTRODUCTION BY

WILL MURRAY

ILLUSTRATIONS BY

JOHN FLEMING GOULD

ALTUS
PRESS

BOSTON • 2018

TABLE OF CONTENTS

INTRODUCTION
WILL MURRAY

PAUL FREDERICK ERNST (1899–1985) cut his fiction-writing teeth on the horror genre, and even after he transitioned to detective-mystery stories, he rarely strayed very far from his macabre roots.

Weird Tales was Ernst's primary market during the 1920s and into the 30s. He sold a fair amount of super-science stuff to Hugo Gernsback's *Amazing Stories* and other fledgling science fiction pulps. Essentially, the Ohio-born pulpster was writing the bottom-paying genre magazines while he worked as an advertising copywriter in Chicago.

Predictably, Ernst broke into Popular Publications via its horror pulps, beginning with *Dime Mystery Magazine* in 1934, reportedly under the names George Edson and George Alden Edson. *Terror Tales* and *Horror Stories* also welcomed him with open arms.

When *Detective Tales* started in 1935, he was present in the first issue. From the start, *Detective Tales* showcased lone-wolf crimebusters conceived as an antidote to the typical tough private eye stories that had been running in *Black Mask* and *Dime Detective* since the late 1920s.

As editor Loring "Dusty" Dowst detailed the new magazine's slant: "Objective, clue-by-clue stories are not wanted. Tales must have action, but at the same time sing with genuine human interest (both sides of the law) warmth, and novelty in plot. This magazine is a sincere effort to re-humanize and re-dramatize the detective story. Our detective tales are based more upon Raffles, Jimmy Valentine, and Jimmy Dale characters than the common-run hard-boiled dick."

O. Henry's Jimmy Valentine and E.W. Hornung's A.J. Raffles belonged to the "gentleman thief" sub-genre popular at the turn of the 20th century. Both were cracks-men—professional safecrackers.

Frank L. Packard's multi-identitied Jimmie Dale, alias the Gray Seal, was an evolution of the breed. He had been popular for over two decades. In one way or another, he served as model for the Depression generation of pulp avengers, including The Shadow and The Spider. A young man about town, Jimmie Dale took to cracking safes for fun, leaving behind a gray paper sticker—the sign of the Gray Seal. He robbed no one, but when a murder is cred-ited to the growing list of the Gray Seal's crimes, he becomes a wanted man. Assuming other underworld identities like Larry the Bat and Smarlinghue the hophead artist, Dale battled real criminals at the behest of a mys-terious blackmailing woman who discovers his secret.

It may not be a coincidence that the first new Gray Seal adventure in five years—*Jimmie Dale and the Missing Hour*—was serialized in *Detective Fiction Weekly* six months prior to the debut of *Detective Tales*.

Paul Ernst's early contribution to the sons of the Gray Seal was the triple-identitied Perry Westbrook, alias The Wraith, the hero of "My Business of Death." His sign of the Eye was pure Jimmie Dale. With his strange pipelike pistol, exotic throwing dagger, and partially paralyzed face, he is a clear and startling forerunner to Street & Smith's The Avenger, whom Ernst would not write until 1939.

When *Strange Detective Mysteries* was launched in the Fall of 1937, under the editorship of Moran Tudary, it made to order for Paul Ernst. His bizarre hero Seekay appeared in the first two issues, and promised to be a regular or semi-regular feature.

"I am looking for unusual detective lead characters," Editorial Director Rogers Terrill explained. "The hero may have an unusual background, or a strange reason for being a detective. He may have some character peculiarities or even a physical deformity. Or he may be engaged in some odd vocation which he makes use of in the detective work."

The enigmatic Seekay stood out from this wild pack. With his disfigured face concealed by a celluloid shield, he might have been inspired by the earliest depictions of The Shadow, of whom creator Walter B. Gibson hinted had suffered a severe facial disfigurement during the First World War. Gibson soon dropped that backstory, but real-life veterans of that terrible conflict who had been damaged in the face were often fitted with celluloid shields or primitive prosthetics in order to live semi-normal lives. Detective Seekay wore both.

While Ernst never supplied any concrete hints of Seekay's history, it's possible that the black-haired mystery man was a veteran of the Great War. Certainly readers of that era would have suspected so. Ernst set these stories in Chicago, with which he was intimately familiar.

As for Seekay's true name, that too remained a deep mystery. One might speculate that it's a play on the word seek—which no doubt it is—but it may also contain a clue to his last name. For Seekay can be read as a pig-Latin-style inversion of the name Casey. Yet it may be simply a phonetic pronunciation of the common initials, C.K.

Strange Detective Mysteries attempted to carve out a new niche in the pulp detective magazine lists—something like a cross between *Dime Detective* and *Dime Mystery's* terror slant, but without the wild semi-supernatural elements and the sex and sadism.

This was the start of that sub-genre branded "Defective Detectives." *Dime Mystery Magazine* made a specialty of these bizarre types. The field included blind sleuths, hemophiliac detectives and sundry maimed and crippled others. They were an attempt to break away from the typical hard-boiled dick stereotypes that had dominated the detective field since the late 1920s. Seekay was one of the pioneers.

Paul Ernst rarely spoke of himself in print. No substantial biography exists of his personal life. So the psychic roots of his many cold-blooded emotionally empty protagonists remains unknown. Whether or not tragedy ever touched his life, at the time these tales were written, he was happily married and living in a converted Pennsylvania farmhouse. And he did once admit, "Honestly, I've never done anything more violent than running out of tobacco in a blizzard and having to walk to Bill White's store, a mile away."

Today, Paul Ernst is best remembered for penning *The Avenger* under the house name of Kenneth Robeson. But going back to his first detective heroes, Ernst was writing similar characters—short, compact but powerfully muscled, these sleuths often wore gray, possessed colorless eyes and masklike, expressionless faces, which rarely betrayed their seething emotions. Ernst often described them as human machines—cold, remorseless manhunters who never failed to get their quarry.

MADAM MURDER—AND THE CORPSE BRIGADE

NONE KNEW WHAT LAY BEHIND SEEKAY'S MASK—SAVE THAT HE HAD NO FACE! YET THOSE RAZOR-SHARP EYES COULD READ THE RED RIDDLE BROUGHT HIM BY A GRIEF-STRICKEN GIRL. HER BROTHER HAD BEEN MURDERED BY A STRANGE WOMAN'S LOVE AND SEEKAY, ALONE, COULD TRAP THAT GRIM BRIGADE OF BLOND BUTCHERS WHO HAD PLAYED CUPID TO THE CORPSE!

CHAPTER ONE
THE MAN WHO
HAD NO FACE

IN THE vestibule door there was a large panel of glass. But the glass was not transparent; it was a mirror. In it, Marian Ford saw her reflection. A young, attractive girl with tawny brown hair under a smart-looking hat, and with dark, frightened blue eyes in a white, drawn, but pretty face.

She instinctively tidied a wisp of hair, and tried to make her face look less horrified. But she couldn't. She was frightened numb, and nothing she could do could conceal it.

She pressed the bell under the single name, *Seekay,* and waited for a buzzer to open the vestibule door. None did. Instead, a voice, deep and measured and powerful, seemed to speak up from under her feet. Its awful suddenness amazed her.

"Come in."

She looked down. The vestibule floor was tile, in a checker design. She saw no place where a voice could have sounded.

She walked to the door, and drew back with a frightened gasp. It was slowly swinging open, revealing a wide hall. And there was no hand behind the door to move it.

   She entered the hall. The door, equally mysteriously and
silently, swung shut again. She bit her lip as she walked
down the ball toward an open doorway through which
light from the street lamp was coming.

   It was all very startling, and yet, somehow, about what
she had expected.

The dark beauty in lounging pajamas
was in the hall—her gun spoke.

"See Seekay," Detective Grann had told her at headquarters. "There's nothing we can do about your case.
Doesn't even sound like you've got a case. Kind of… crazy…
if you'll pardon my saying so. Well, Seekay is kind of crazy,
too. But he's a good private dick, at that. See him."

So she was here to lay her case before Seekay. And she
was already tasting some of the bizarre incidents in store

for visitors to that bizarre house in Chicago's near North Side.

"In here, please," a voice sounded from the room ahead of her. The same deep, powerful voice that had sounded in the vestibule.

MARIAN FORD turned into the room. It was dark save for the light from the street raying in the high, un-shaded windows. In that dim and tricky light she saw walls lined with books, a great desk, and at the desk a figure that was so much in shadow that all she could see about it was that it was masculine.

This was in line with what Detective Grann had hinted, too. "Seekay keeps himself in the dark pretty much. You probably won't see him clearly—unless he takes on your case. Which I doubt," the detective had added. "He isn't doing much now."

The figure at the desk spoke, remaining as motionless as a wax dummy.

"You are terribly frightened. Be at ease. Tell me what happened to you at the hospital."

Marian gasped. "How did you know I had been to a hospital?"

Seekay's deep voice was impatient.

"I have a nose, and the smell of a hospital persists in clothing. You learned something there that upset you, and you went to the police. They sent you here."

"My brother," said Marian, her senses beginning to reel again in the terror that had sent her here. "He has brain fever. He is raving. Nonsense. But the most horrible non-sense! Delirious stuff that sounds mad—but which I feel somehow has meaning. Some one has done something dreadful to him. I know they have. Because just last week

I got a letter from him in which he seemed to be exceptionally well, and very happy. In fact, he was going to be married.

"Then, this afternoon, I get a wire from the North Side Emergency Hospital saying that he is very ill and I am to come at once. I got there to find him completely broken, raving, mad! Some horrible recent experience is responsible. And I want to find out what it was."

FROM THE dim figure, came musingly: "Delirious raving usually uses true words. It is broken truth, which can mean a great deal if it can be pieced together. What does he say?"

The girl shuddered.

"He says, over and over again, 'Dead men kill.' And then he mutters about being attacked by a dead man. He describes the... the corpse. Blond, tall, thin, blue-eyed, with a scar on its forehead. And he winds up with the same insane statement: 'Dead men kill.... Dead men kill. Dead—'"

"You are not from Chicago," said the dim figure.

"How...." The girl stopped. "Oh. Yes. I told you I had received a wire from the hospital, didn't I?"

"There is more than that to tell me you're from out of town. There is a sharp crease down the side of your spring coat. You have been seated in the same position for a long time—probably, several hours. In a bus or train. A bus, almost certainly—in a train you would have taken off your coat."

"I just came by bus from Fontayne, a small town north of Milwaukee."

"Your name?"

"Marian Ford. My brother's name is Charles Ford. I haven't seen him for nearly a year. We haven't been very close since he left home ten years ago. Now we are each other's only relatives."

"You say he has been in excellent health till just now, when you found him in Emergency Hospital with brain fever?"

"As far as I know, yes." Marian's hands clenched. "Something terrible has happened to him."

"Something might have happened which was terrible but not in the least criminal. What does your brother do?"

"He has a job with the Chicago National Bank. Not a very big job. He's only a teller there."

"You say he recently married?"

"I said he intended to be married, according to the letter he wrote last week. It might be that that has something to do with his dangerous illness."

"It might be that it has," said Seekay slowly.

"Perhaps the girl he meant to marry threw him down at the last minute—"

"I think," said Seekay dryly, "that it must be more serious than that. I don't believe a broken engagement would land a man in a hospital with brain fever."

"It… doesn't sound reasonable…. Will you investigate, at least a little, and try to find out what's wrong?"

" 'Dead men kill'," quoted Seekay softly. "That is odd enough to appeal even to me. I am going to turn on the light now. Do not be alarmed at my face."

Marian felt a tingle touch her spine. Since first setting foot into the room she had wondered why its occupant, the almost mythical Seekay, had chosen to remain in darkness. Was he a monster of some sort? A gruesome freak? Maimed, deformed? What? Why had the men at police headquarters looked so uneasy at the mention of Seekay's name?

The lights in the room flashed on suddenly, and in spite of the warning, Marian barely managed to turn a soft scream into a gasp as her eyes rested on the face of the man she had been talking to.

No, that is inaccurate. Her eyes didn't rest on his face—because Seekay had no face. Where a face should have been there was a blank curve of something pink and softly shining, like celluloid, extending from the hairline down to a point just under where a chin should be.

Through this half cylinder of plastic substance that shielded Seekay, stared black eyes that were like jet with little fires in them. Over the gruesome shield was thick, virile black hair shot with gray streaks. Under it was a tall, powerful body immaculately clad in grey spring flannels.

Everything normal, crisp, even attractive looking, except for the hideous blank where a face should have been.

But why was it blank? What dreadful disfigurement did Seekay hide under the half-cylinder of celluloid?

Marian had recovered from the shock of Seekay's bizarre, unexpected appearance.

"I could have let you see me first in the guise I assume when I leave my house," Seekay said calmly. "But I am afraid that is almost as bad as this. However, if you will pardon me, I shall go and change to it."

He left the room, returning in a short time with a low-brimmed hat on, and a topcoat over his arm. Gloves and stick were in his right hand.

He had a face now. It was lean, impassive, with odd linelessness around the eyes. Also, it was oddly hairless. Marian gasped again, after a moment, as she saw that this face was as artificial as the celluloid shield. It was a mask, too; marvelously designed to look like life, but failing of course as all such attempts fail under a second glance. Again she wondered what terrible malformation made such shielding necessary. But her wonder died in a return of her original horror, of which she was reminded when Seekay spoke.

"Come. We'll go to the hospital and see if we can help your brother."

CHAPTER TWO

THE DEAD HAVE SECRETS

IT WAS almost midnight, but Seekay's name made mock of rules like hospital visiting hours. He and Marian were led along a dim corridor lined with rooms in which patients were sleeping—or longing vainly for sleep—to a room at the rear.

In this room a young man lay in bed. At first he looked normal. Then you saw the flush on his face, the feverish brightness of his eyes when they opened to glare emptily, and the way his hands picked aimlessly at the bedclothes. Marian ran to the bed with a low cry. The nurse sitting beside Charles Ford in the feeble illumination of a night-light, shook her head warningly. Seekay walked in.

The nurse stared at his face, looked again, with growing comprehension and shock in her eyes, then veiled her expression. Seekay paid no attention. He must have long ago become accustomed to such starts of surprise, almost of fear, from people gazing for the first time on his face-lessness.

Seekay went at once to the bed. With a physician's deftness, he slid up one of the sick man's eyelids. The lid jerked and quivered and remained almost as widely open when it was released.

The man began to mumble. Seekay bent nearer his lips.

"Dead men…." Charles Ford was muttering. "Dead men…."

Seekay's black eyes glittered in the smooth-fitting eye-holes of his lifelike mask.

"Yes," he murmured. "Dead men. What do they do?"

"You haven't said you loved me. Dollar for dollar. Dead men."

"What do the dead men do?" repeated Seekay softly.

The night nurse stared with narrowed eyes. Plainly, she had been sure the patient was hopelessly out of his mind. And plainly she suspected the man in the painted mask to be equally out of his mind for trying to take seriously such mad words.

"Kill. Dead men kill." Charles Ford's face became more blood-suffused. His eyes were suddenly lakes of horror. "Dead men kill. One chased me. You are so beautiful. After me. Closer, ever closer. Dollar for dollar, as you said. Red leather floor."

"Where did the dead man chase you?" whispered Seekay. "Where? Where?" His voice was compelling, if low. "Tell us where he chased you."

"House in the trees. Dollar for dollar, as you said. You are so beautiful. Dead men…."

Ford's voice died. He stared rigidly upward. Seekay turned to the nurse.

"Know anything about him?"

"Not much. The desk said an old man by the name of Amos Keller brought him in. He picked him up on the highway, north, near Lake Forest. The man was staggering as if he was drunk, Keller said. But he had a hunch he was sick. He discovered just how sick on his ride down to the city, and he stopped by here and had us take him in. That was at four this afternoon. He hasn't been rational since."

"Picked him up near Lake Forest," Seekay repeated.

MARIAN SUDDENLY bent closer. She had been watching her brother's eyes. And now, for the first time, she saw in them a faint flicker of reason. Ford's face, from being blood-suffused, had suddenly become alarmingly pale.

"Lake Forest," he whispered. "Yes. Yes! Lake Forest! The grey house—"

His voice stopped. He had been straining up from the pillow. He fell back now.

"Oh," gasped Marian, in a thin, frightened voice. "Oh, my God!"

The nurse elbowed Seekay out of the way and caught at Ford's wrist. Seekay said grimly, "No use. He's dead. Poison of some sort. Killed to keep him from talking."

"He couldn't have been poisoned," said the nurse, trembling as she faced the jet-black eyes. "I've been in here with him every minute—"

"Alone?" Seekay shot out.

"Well, no. Not all the time. A Doctor Blount, his personal physician, came in about a half hour ago—"

"He didn't have such a thing as a personal physician," cried Marian. "He's never been sick in his life. I doubt if he even knew a doctor here!"

"The man said he was Mr. Ford's personal physician—"

"He was Ford's executioner," Seekay said grimly. "What did he look like?"

"He was tall, blue-eyed, blond. He had a thin scar on his forehead. Right in the center." She clasped her hands together.

The description wrung an exclamation from Marian. "The same description Charles gave to the dead man he said chased him! What *is* this, anyway?"

Seekay turned on her the gruesomely lifelike mask that shielded whatever sort of features were his own.

"Something big is behind this. And you were right—something terrible did happen to your brother. He was murdered to keep him from speaking about it. I only hope he's not the only one."

IN SEEKAY'S big coupe, Marian cried a little. "I hadn't see him much since we were both kids. He didn't write very often, or keep in touch. But after all he was my brother," she faltered, as though in defense of tears that certainly needed no defending.

Seekay said nothing at all. He drove north, block after block, with what he used for a face staring straight ahead over the wheel of the powerful coupe. And finally, as they got far north in Chicago's suburbs, Marian got control of herself.

"Crying won't do much good, will it? After all, the job is to find who killed my brother.... If you will take it on?"

Seekay nodded.

"We haven't much to go on," said Marian forlornly.

"We have a great deal to go on. All the statements of your brother, for instance."

"But they were delirious—crazy—"

"I always accept as truth the statements I hear made from delirium. Distorted, perhaps—but true. And what were your brother's statements? 'Dead men kill. Chased me. House in the trees. Dollar for dollar. You are so beautiful. Grey house in Lake Forest. Red leather floor.'"

"But nobody could guess at the meaning of those things!" Marian exclaimed. "A house in the trees! That couldn't possibly mean anything." She stared at him.

"You have picked the one statement that is easily deciphered. House in the trees. That is easy."

Seekay swung over the Lake Forest line and sped to a small-house section west of the tracks. He stopped before one, stared at the number.

"Two eighty-three. This is Amos Keller's house. Keller was with your brother for an hour or more, while he was driving him in to the city. He may have invaluable information for us—if he is in a position to give it to us!"

Marian looked at the place, and a little chill of premonition coursed down her spine. The house, a small white clapboard structure, was in darkness. Natural, since it was after one in the morning. But there was something eerie about that darkness....

Seekay had gotten out. He started toward the front door. He didn't say anything about her staying in the car, so she got out and went with him. He knocked.

There was no answer. For a moment Seekay stared at the blank and unresponsive door. His mask, like a thing worn in a play, hiding sadness or ecstasy, grief or joy in a rigid immobility, increased the eeriness of the moment. Then he got out a small leather case, drew a slim tool from it, and a moment later walked into the house.

They hadn't to search far for the man from whom they had hoped to get information. They found him in the front room, within ten feet of the door. Marian bit her lips to keep from shrieking, and shrank behind Seekay's powerful figure.

Amos Keller, a mild-looking man of sixty-five or so, dressed in well-worn black, lay on the floor in a sprawled heap. The blue hole between his eyes was so inconspicuous that it hardly detracted from the serenity into which his features relaxed in death. Marian tried not to look at the red pool that had seeped from the back of his head. It was drying.

Seekay bent over the body. Marian felt like screaming at the emotionlessness of that mask. It made Seekay seem like a machine, a robot, staring on death or life, tragedy or felicity, with uncomprehending woodenness.

THERE WERE powder-burns on the forehead. The shot had been fired from close range. Seekay lifted the dead man's hands carefully. He drew out a lens and stared at them, then cautiously picked something from the nail of the right forefinger. Marian saw it—a single, short hair. He put this in a tiny blank envelope.

"Amos Keller will never tell us anything in words," he said, his voice issuing uncannily from the unmoving slit of his painted mouth. "But in death he may tell us more than he would have thought he could."

"He was killed, as Charles was, to keep him from talking?" she said.

Seekay nodded. He strode to a telephone in the hall, and got the Lake Forest police. He reported the murder in crisp, metallic words, hung up as questions began to be shot at him, and drew Marian toward the door.

"We can do no good here. And personal contact with the police will only delay us."

They started south. Marian felt cold and weak. Two men, one of them her own brother, killed in some mysterious business the sole key to which was her brother's delirious babble!

Seekay talked, as though more to himself than to her.

"*Rigor mortis* just starting. Some blood clotted, a bit still liquid. Keller was killed about two hours and a half ago. Not less than two or more than three, I should say. That makes Keller's murder happen at about the same time your brother was given poison at the hospital. The powder-burn shows close contact. The hair from under Keller's nail confirms that. He had his hands on the killer, clawing and fighting when he saw the gun."

Marian only half heard. They got to Seekay's house.

At the front and side of the place, next to the regular street door, was a big sliding-door. Seekay switched his lights on and off twice, and the door opened silently, worked by some double photo-electric cell device. He drove the car in. The door closed behind them.

"Wait in here," he said a moment later.

Marian found herself in the room where she had first talked to Seekay. He went to an adjoining room, leaving the door open. She saw that it was a small laboratory.

She saw him bend studiously over a microscope, then saw intense light ray out in a tiny focal point. He came back. The mask only excited Marian's compassion now. She was no longer startled or disquieted by it.

"Keller was killed by a blond man who touched up his blondness with peroxide," Seekay said crisply. " 'Dead men kill….' I shouldn't wonder if this blond murderer has a scar on his forehead."

MARIAN'S EYES widened. "But that would be the description given by the nurse of the 'doctor' who came in to see my brother! And you say he was given poison at about the same time Keller was killed!"

"At approximately the same time. Certainly within a half hour."

"No one could possibly get from the near North Side of Chicago to Lake Forest in half an hour," protested Marian.

"That's right," nodded Seekay absently.

"Then how in the world—"

He held tip his hand for silence. There was a soft buzzing. Marian recognized it—the sound of the front doorbell.

Seekay stepped to the desk. There was a small black box on it. He clicked a little switch and stared at a frosted-glass plate.

"A simple development of television," he said. "In this I can see who is at my door, through the glass panel."

"But the panel is a mirror," said Marian.

"A mirror on the outside only, opaque from that angle, but as transparent as window glass from the inside. A crude trick, but effective. Would you like to see our caller?"

Marian stepped to the little box and stared at the plate. There was a tiny picture on it now, and her blood ran cold as she stared.

The picture was of a man. Blond, tall, thin, with ice-blue eyes. There was a scar on his forehead.

"My brother's murderer!" she whispered.

"Perhaps," shrugged Seekay. He touched a button, and the figure suddenly disappeared. At the same time they heard a far shout of alarm.

"There is a convenient little cell under the vestibule floor," said Seekay calmly. "A spring catch tilts the floor and deposits undesirable visitors in it. Again, crude but effective. I'll call my friend, Grann, at headquarters, and we'll have this man locked up. He'll have a silenced gun with him. That will hold him for a while."

"He came here to—"

"To kill us," nodded Seekay easily. "The brain that traced your brother to the hospital via Keller's car, has discovered that I am on the case. And I am to be silenced. You, too."

Marian's hands clenched.

"This will probably he the last attempt on our lives tonight," he said. "But just the same, perhaps you had better stay here for the present. You'll be safer."

"In the morning?" said Marian.

"In the morning," said Seekay, "we shall locate the 'house in the trees' and start working from there. So dead men kill, eh? Somebody has the brain of the devil himself!"

CHAPTER THREE
HOUSE IN THE SKY

AN IMPERTURBABLE man-servant served breakfast to Marian at nine. She went downstairs and to the big room Seekay had fitted up as an office. He was there, behind his great desk.

He had the plain celluloid shield over his face again— the one she had seen him in first. Evidently, he preferred that to the more human-looking mask he wore when outside of his house. Perhaps, she thought, the looser, blanker shield was less hot and irritating to whatever formation of flesh lay underneath.

"Good morning," Seekay nodded, turning his faceless-ness toward her as she came in the door. "Things have been happening while you had your beauty sleep. A singularly successful sleep, if you don't mind my saying so."

She blushed a little with pleasure, but only said, "What has happened?"

"The gentleman who was so naive as to call at our front door last night, won't go calling any more. I cautioned Grann particularly, when he came to pick him up. But the brain behind all this, got him. Shot through the head, as he was getting out of the squad car at headquarters—to keep him from talking. Grann is sore as the devil, but he says they'll get the killer soon. They have his description from a bystander.

"The killer," Seekay said slowly, "seems to have been a blond man, tall, thin, with a scar on his forehead."

"Just like the man who was killed," whispered Marian.

"Yes."

"Just like the fake doctor who… murdered my brother."

"Yes."

"And like the man who—if that hair means anything—murdered Keller at about the same time, thirty miles north."

"Yes."

"What does it mean?" burst out Marian.

"The key is in your brother's statement, 'Dead men kill.'" Seekay ruffled some papers. "But more has happened than murder. I've been phoning real-estate agencies in the north suburbs, and also classified advertising departments of newspapers. I've found out two very interesting things. One concerns the house in the trees."

"There *is* such a thing?"

"Oh, distinctly. I had an idea what it might be as soon as the nurse told us your brother had been picked up, dazed, in Lake Forest. On the south township line, next to the lake, there is a tree of immense size and spread. In the lower branches of that tree, for a novelty, somebody built a small dancing pavilion and a bar. A sort of tree night club. I believe it was called the Owl's Club. I remembered having seen that, but couldn't place it. The real-estate people told me where it was." Seekay's long, strong fingers made an arch. "The place is empty and abandoned, now. The Lake Forest residents managed to have it shut up under their residence zoning restrictions."

"You think—Charles was there?"

"Yes. 'Dead men kill. Chased me. House in the trees.' That's pretty plain. Your brother escaped from something, so alarming that it rocked his reason, to that abandoned treehouse. So far so good. Now, you told me your brother worked in a bank?"

Marian nodded.

"Which bank, please?"

"The Chicago National."

Seekay dialed a number on his phone, spoke briefly for a moment, then turned to Marian with his black eyes grim in the eyeholes of his fantastic shield.

HE SAID: "Prepare yourself for a shock, Miss Ford. Your brother embezzled money from the bank yesterday. A great deal of money. Something over a hundred thousand dollars. The examiners are checking now, after which the theft will be made public."

"He didn't! Charles was no thief! Oh, my God—he didn't!"

Seekay's eyes were pitying. "I don't believe he was. That theft was part of this whole hellish set-up. Don't look like that.... Let's see if we can't clear his name before we get through."

Marian sat down again, gasping.

Seekay said musingly, " 'Dollar for dollar.' The embezzlement is connected with that. We have four mysterious statements left. 'You are so beautiful. Grey house in Lake Forest. Red leather floor.' And, of course, the key of all, 'Dead men kill.' You told me your brother had written a gay letter about intending to be married. The beauty must refer to that."

He got up from the desk. "The grey house in Lake Forest comes next. Somewhere near the tree-house, of course. I'll have something to report to you soon—"

Marian's hands clenched. This was a moment for which she had steeled herself. "I want to go with you."

"Impossible, I'm afraid. I expect to find the grey house. I expect to find in it an answer to what happened to your brother. Also in that house will be—death."

"You don't expect to die, do you?"

"Naturally not. I have cheated death before. I think I can cheat it again."

"Then you can cheat it for two." Marian rushed on before he could say anything: "My brother was killed! Poisoned, after being horribly mistreated in some way! I want to help get justice for that with my own hands! Don't refuse me!"

The blank mask turned toward the window.

"It will be very dangerous, Miss Ford. But I can understand your feelings. I'll take you, if you will do just as I tell you to, without question."

A QUARTER of an hour till noon. The spring sun beat down on the two. They sat in the coupe for a moment before a house by the lake in lower Lake Forest. The house was of grey rough stone; the only grey house for many blocks. It was a block and a half from the abandoned Owl's

Club, which could be seen across the well-kept lawns of several estates intervening.

"This is it," said Seekay, with quiet conviction.

"It looks like the respectable home of some respectable family of wealth," objected Marian. "What are you going to do now?"

"Walk in," said Seekay.

"Just—walk in? If that house is the murder nest it seems to be, they'll have noticed your car out here in front. They'll know who you are and all about you. They'll try to kill you."

"Us," Seekay corrected calmly.

"But—"

"I told you it would be dangerous. But I think I can take care of us. You see, the average killer's mind works in a one-way track. He tends to kill always in the same way—the way in which he first succeeded. I mean to let this blond man with the scar on his forehead try to kill us, and from the method solve the last bits of this puzzle."

"The last bits?"

"Yes. I believe I have it all in my mind now, except for the part about a dead man killing. That, which impressed your brother most of all, doesn't yet make sense to me."

"The red leather floor?" said Marian.

"That doesn't seem to say anything, either. But I don't think it's of much importance. Come on."

He walked toward the house, across a flagged path from the gate to the small porch.

"What are you going to say to get us in here?" asked Marian. Her knees felt weak. But she wasn't showing it. She had a great deal of faith in the faceless detective.

"I'm going to say I'm a private detective, here to ask about Charles Ford, and that you're his sister."

"But, my God—"

"The best attack is usually the direct attack. In this case particularly, since we probably can get no proof of murder till murder has also been tried on us."

The house, set in a quarter-block of lawn, looked beautifully serene. There were flower beds artistically placed. Murder seemed very far off. But that it was not far off was attested by the way Marian's heart pumped with instinctive terror. Wild bells of alarm were ringing deep in her breast.

Seekay calmly lifted the knocker on the door and let it clang down. The reverberation of it echoed through the house.

"You may get a shock when this door is opened," Seekay said in a low tone. "Don't show it too much—"

The door was swung smoothly back. A man in butler's livery stood in the door. His face was bland, and he was prosaic in every detail. But Marian felt a surge of horror pass over her.

The servant was tall, thin, blond, blue-eyed, with a scar on his forehead!

CHAPTER FOUR
BEHIND THE MASK

IN EVERY detail, he was the man who had stood in Seekay's vestibule last night, and had been arrested a little later by Detective Grann. The only difference was that last night he had worn topcoat and derby hat, and today he wore butler's rig.

But the man who had called last night was dead!

Could it be—

"Yes?" the butler said, in expressionless inquiry.

"I'd like to speak to the master of the house, please," said Seekay.

"Yes, sir. Who shall I tell him is calling?"

"Private Detective Seekay, and Miss Marian Ford."

"Yes, sir." The butler's blue eyes were like glass. They dwelt curiously on the painted face Seekay wore over his facial expanse, but that was all.

Seekay and Marian stood in a broad, luxuriously furnished hall while the man walked upstairs. Then, from a room at the left, footsteps sounded.

A woman stepped into the hall. She was young, not more than twenty-eight. She was unusually beautiful, with great dark eyes, blue-black hair and a flawless skin. Her figure was something to catch a man's breath; and a good deal of it could be seen. Marian's eyebrows drew together at the sheerness of her pale-blue lounging pajamas.

"I couldn't help hearing you announce yourself," she said, smiling thinly. "A detective? To see my brother? May I ask why?"

"I came here to ask after a certain Charles Ford," Seekay said calmly. "This young lady's brother. He was hurt, and is at present in Emergency Hospital. He was seen near here. I wanted to ask if he had been at this house."

"Charles Ford?" repeated the dark beauty, eyes widening. "I'm quite sure no such person has been here. Not to my knowledge, at least. But perhaps my brother knows. Won't you come to his study and wait for him?"

Marian's heart was thudding faster. Danger! Danger! But she took her cue from the faceless man beside her who said, "Of course. We'll wait wherever you like."

The woman walked down the hall. Marian followed on numb legs, looking up sidewise at Seekay's painted face. His black eyes held no more expression than his mask.

"Here, if you please," said the woman pleasantly.

She put her hand on the knob of a closed door, Seekay and Marian walked close. Seekay drew Marian into the room. She had just a glimpse of a curious, Chinese red floor, and then the door pounded into place behind them and a lock clicked.

MARIAN CLUTCHED at Seekay's arm. Her breath was beginning to choke her now. "The door! It's locked! We're trapped in here!" Couldn't he see the danger?

Seekay nodded. "Yes, I thought we would be. Excellent!"

"But we'll be killed—"

"Not for a little while, at least," said Seekay calmly. "Our lovely hostess and her brother, if he is her brother, will check very carefully for a time to see if we were really stupid enough to come here alone. After that, he will return. Meanwhile, we'll look around—"

Marian interrupted him with a scream. She had seen, protruding from beyond a long table at the far end of the room, a sprawled leg.

They went swiftly to the table. And once more Marian felt ice seem to form around her thudding heart. There was a dead man there. *And he was blond, tall, thin, with glazed blue eyes and a scar on his forehead!*

It was all Marian could do to keep from fainting. This man had killed her brother. He had killed Keller at about the same time in another place. He had been killed after Grann had arrested him. He had seemed to let them into this house. Now he lay here, dead! She could feel her reason trembling. She felt like babbling delirious phrases as her brother had....

"Dead men kill," quoted Seekay softly, looking at that dead face. "Dead for many hours. Your brother saw this dead man, and a little later saw what seemed the same man, trying to kill him. The night was too crowded with emergencies, because of your brother's escape and their efforts to silence him and us, to allow them to get rid of this body."

He turned from the corpse, and looked speculatively at the carpetless floor of the room which was scantily furnished as a library. And the floor, itself, was of some sort of dully gleaming, glassy plastic, colored brilliant red.

"The execution chamber," mused Seekay, with his voice as cold as glacial floes. "Clever. It doesn't matter how much blood is spilled in here. This synthetic flooring can be scrubbed, easily, so clean that a microscope couldn't find traces of blood. That gets rid of one of the big perils of murder—bloodstains. These people are certainly in the business."

"It looks... like red patent leather," quavered Marian.

Seekay nodded. "That explains the red leather floor.... Tell me, what does the phrase, 'dollar for dollar' mean to you?"

"I've only heard it in connection with a sort of proposed partnership," said Marian. Shuddering, she wondered if their host hadn't about made sure they had come here alone, and wasn't ready now to turn his deadly attention on them. " 'I'll match you dollar for dollar. I'll give dollar for dollar with you.' That's the way I've heard the phrase used."

Seekay nodded, with eyes like glittering jet in the eyeholes of the painted face.

"Of course. And that's the way it was used here. An old crime trick but still good."

HE SAID: "Your brother, teller in a bank, fell in love with the dark beauty who ushered us in here. She lives in a fine home, seems wealthy. Your brother protests at marrying money. His sweetheart's brother, who says he has taken a great liking to him, draws him aside and offers to give him, as a sort of equalizing dowry, dollar for dollar a sum matching whatever he can show in the way of a fortune. Your brother falls for the trick, and walks out of the bank with a large sum of money. When he has shown it to the elder brother of the girl he loves, and has gotten the offered amount matching it, he can then return the borrowed money to the bank.

"He come out here with the borrowed cash, and shows it to the girl's brother. Then the precious pair coolly murder him, and take the money, and plant his body so that it will seem that he has committed suicide in a fit of remorse over his 'embezzlement.' At least that was the plan, and God knows on how many poor young devils they've worked it successfully. But your brother escaped, to die later of poisoning in Emergency Hospital."

Marian stared at the dead man for a shuddering moment.

"But this man we seem to see, now alive, now dead—"

"When you plan a series of crimes," said Seekay, "you plan first to hide your identity. The usual way is to disguise yourself. The cold-blooded devil behind this crime series had another way. One that was revealed by a study of recent classified advertising.

"He got several men, blond, blue-eyed, tall, thin, about like himself, on the pretext of wanting them as servants. If they weren't quite blond enough, he touched them up with peroxide; the facial resemblance was most important. Not too great a resemblance, either. If you saw any two of these men together, you'd see their differences. But they were enough alike so that descriptions would tally of various men committing various crimes at about the same time.

"Since no man can be in two places at the same moment, the profusion of identical descriptions would work as an alibi. It would make legal identity almost impossible, in case his plan slipped up.

"Some of his blond dummies either were crooks to start with, or turned crooked in his employ. But I believe others were honest. This man in here probably was—saw something he shouldn't have seen, and was killed. A little later your brother was thrown in here, saw him, and then was apparently attacked by the same man—whom he knew was dead. Hence, 'Dead men kill. Chased me. House in the trees.' It was not an illusion deliberately manufactured for your brother's benefit, but it was one he would naturally get, and it rocked his mind."

Seekay was taking off his grey flannel suit-coat as he spoke. He moved with it to the room's one window, through which daylight was streaming.

"Our turn will come very soon now. We'd better make a few preparations. Take off that spring suit of yours, please."

MARIAN GASPED in surprise. Then she checked the questions crowding her lips and, with the implicit obedience she had promised before coming here with him, she took off the knee-length tweed coat she wore, and the short, chic suit-coat underneath it. With the short coat came a frilled dicky that filled in its V.

"They won't try to shoot us from the door," she heard his calm musing, as he indulged in his trick of talking more to himself than to her. "They can be sure I have a gun and will be watching the door. Some concealed panel in one of the walls. We'll trick them with darkness...."

Marian's fingers were numbly working with the snaps on her skirt. It fell in a ring around her feet as Seekay stepped up on the sill of the window.

"Pins?"

She had two, safety pins. With them, Seekay fastened his coat to the drapes at the top of the window. The coat curtained the window for about a third of its length.

"Your clothes, please."

Marian stepped to the window, shrinking a little from the hard light that revealed that under the three-piece tweed suit there had been near-nakedness. She stood on tiptoe, with lithe straight legs stretched as she handed him the garments. She had no more pins, but in her long bob were several hairpins. With those, Seekay fastened her garments to his coat.

The window was completely shrouded, plunging the room into the dimness of late dusk.

"This might disquiet you," said Seekay, leaving the window and walking toward the dead man by the desk. "I'd suggest that you look the other way for a moment."

She turned, a slender white statue in the dimness. She heard Seekay moving near the desk.

"All right, now."

She turned back. She saw Seekay kneeling on his heels, leaning back against the low bulk of the desk, facing the door. The dim light barely revealed his painted mask, under the hat pulled low over his forehead. His right hand was by his side as he stared, without moving a muscle, at the door.

But then his voice sounded, and it came from beyond the desk!

"Lie down in the corner, there. That will put you as much out of the line of fire as possible, no matter where it comes from."

Ventriloquism? she wondered in astonishment. Or were her eyes playing tricks on her? Then she saw the ruse.

Seekay had propped the corpse there against the desk, and had put over the dead face his own painted mask, with his own hat above it. He, himself, lurked behind the desk. That meant that for the first time since she had met Seekay, he had his own countenance—whatever it might be—exposed.

She lay down, hugging the corner.

The waiting—for a murderous attack that might come at once or not for an hour—set her to gnawing at her lip till the blood almost came. She didn't see how they had a chance, here in a locked room, with a panel to open very shortly at some unknown spot from which the killer could cut them down.

They waited.... And then steps out in the hall, by the door, came to their ears. Marian glanced at the desk, behind which Seekay crouched. He had been wrong. They meant to shoot from the door after all....

COINCIDENTAL WITH the loud steps, there was the faintest imaginable noise from the wall almost above where Marian lay. And then three shots snapped out—and the body propped at the desk jerked three times and fell.

And one more shot roared, not from the wall but from behind the desk.

There was a terrific *spang-g-g* of metal in the small square opening in the wall above Marian, a wild drumming of feet on the other side of the wall, and a crash. A woman's scream ripped out.

Seekay leaped from behind the desk. And Marian had a thought which, under the deadly circumstances, was utterly mad. *Now—I shall see his face!* That was the crazy notion that occupied her mind in spite of death, and the threat of death, all around her. But Seekay had his hands over his face. Almost in one move he leaped to the dead man who had taken his bullets, ripped the mask off, turned from Marian, and swung back with it securely in its accustomed place again. Then he leaped to the door and began pouring shots through the lock.

He banged it open. Marian ran into the hall with him.

The dark beauty in lounging pajamas was in the hall. Her eyes were mad with fear and rage. There was a gun in her hand. All the potential deadliness Marian had sensed in her was on the surface now. Her gun spoke, as Seekay whirled.

But the second time, the slug from it ripped down into the floor, as the gun fell from a hand which was no longer a tapered, delicate, white instrument of murder, but a grotesque mass wrenched and dislocated by the force with which the gun had been torn from her fingers by Seekay's unerring bullet.

The blond butler was crouching by the steps. Seekay covered him.

"Get the police," Seekay said. Then, without even looking at him any more, he turned and went into the room adjoining that which had been a death chamber.

In a huddle by a fallen chair, next to the wall, was one more dead man. One more who was blond, thin, tall, blue-eyed. The man they had left behind in the death room, you would have said. There was even part of a scar left on what had been the forehead. Not much was left, though. Seekay's bullet, snapped at the small wall-opening, had hit this man's gun barrel first and ricocheted off into his skull with dreadful shapelessness....

"This is the real one," Seekay said softly. "The master form from which the others were moulded. Your brother has had his revenge."

THE POLICE came. They cuffed the moaning dark-haired woman and the white-faced blond butler. "Go easy on this one," Seekay said, nodding his faceless head toward the servant. "He was just working here for wages."

They sat in the coupe for a moment. Marian glanced from the grim grey house to Seekay's mask. She straightened her skirt.

"You took a dreadful chance when you jumped into the hall after shooting the lock from the door of that room," she said. "Suppose the servant as well as that... that dreadful woman... had been waiting for you out there? You couldn't have escaped *two* guns. One of them would have surely killed you."

Seekay's black eyes played on her.

"I knew the butler wouldn't be there with a gun in his hand. I knew he wasn't in on it at all. Tell me how?"

Marian was thoughtful under the challenge. Then she said slowly, "I think I know. When he let you into the house he showed surprise and curiosity at the sight of your... face."

"Right." She sensed him smiling humorless beneath the mask. "This shielded face of mine is a weapon, in a way. When people show no surprise at it, I know they know all about me and are expecting me. Our lovely hostess showed no surprise, proving instantly that she was ready for my call, was prepared to see me—and to deal with me. The butler did show surprise, indicating that he knew nothing about me, and hence nothing about his employer's murderous affairs. He was an innocent stooge, like the blond in the room with the red floor, who was put out of the way because he had seen too much and had protested."

His black eyes were steady. "You are intelligent, Miss Ford."

Marian drew a deep breath. "I'm glad you think so. Because I…." The words came in a rush. "I'd like to work for you. You need some one."

For a long time Seekay stared at her. Then his eyes smiled if his lips could not.

"Shake," he said, extending his hand.

THE CORPSE WITH THE THIRD EYE

FROM ITS GLASS MUSEUM CASE, BABBLED SEEKAY'S TERRIFIED CLIENT, HAD SPRUNG THAT LONG-DEAD, SACRED WHITE TIGER OF INDIA, ROARING FOR REVENGE AGAINST THE VANDALS WHO HAD DESECRATED ITS FAR-AWAY NATIVE TEMPLE! AND ONLY SEEKAY, WHO HAD NO FACE BUT A BRAIN THAT COULD UNRAVEL MURDER, READ THE TRUE ANSWER MIRRORED IN DEAD MEN'S EYES!

CHAPTER ONE
WHITE TIGER TERROR

I **N THE** near North Side home of that extraordinary and bizarre detective, Seekay, Marian Ford, his private secretary and right-hand man, walked down the short hall to the inner room. She was tall and lithe, strikingly beautiful, with tawny-brown hair worn in a long bob, and deep-blue eyes.

She opened the door of Seekay's private office. The big room was dim, as always, with rich drapes over the street windows to shut out Chicago's rather murky daylight. Marian felt her usual thrill as she stared across the large bare desk at her employer.

Seekay was a tall, powerful man, with long square hands and massive shoulders. His eyes were glittering black—and that was all you could see of his face…. The rest was covered by a blank, rounded shield of pinkish celluloid. Just the half-cylinder of pink, from black hairline to below the chin—that was Seekay's "face." When he went out of the house he wore a mask with nose and mouth painted in, less inhuman looking than the blank cellulloid shield, yet even more ghastly because of the mask's unreality.

"A client…" began Marian.

Seekay nodded, flaming black eyes steady on hers through the eyes holes of the shield. "An East Indian, middle-aged, short, heavy-set, wearing a white turban with a cat's-eye at the center fold. He seems to be thoroughly frightened, though concealing it well, and his fright has infected you though you can't say why."

Marian was not surprised. The tall, attractive girl knew that there was a miniature television system between Seekay's desk and the vestibule of the house. When the

The keen blade sped straight
to Seekay's heart!

bell-button under Seekay's name was pressed it revealed
to the detective the person ringing.

"Bring him in," said Seekay.

Marian went out, returning with the client.

SEEKAY'S GUESS that the Indian was frightened badly, even though concealing it, was confirmed. The man's dark face was immobile and his eyelids didn't flicker. But his complexion was olive-green. He stared hard at the private detective's blank mask, searching into the flaming black eyes which were the only feature showing.

"You are Seekay." It was a statement more than a question.

Seekay nodded, and waited.

"Good," said the Indian, speaking in meticulous English with a slight Oxford accent. "You are very intelligent. Your eyes say so. And you are resourceful. The white tiger may have met his match in you."

It was gibberish to Marian. She didn't see how it could be anything else to Seekay; but the faceless detective did not show surprise.

"You came to see me about a white tiger?" he said. "May I ask—is it the euphonious name of some criminal? Or really a white tiger?" He spoke quietly.

"It is really a white tiger—dead, mounted. But it is not so much with the tiger that I am concerned, as it is with the white tiger's prophecy."

"I see. A dead animal—a white tiger—stuffed and mounted, has prophesied death, so you come to me."

"How did you know it was death that was predicted?"

Seekay waved his hand impatiently. "People only come to me with extreme cases, and with business too unusual for the police to handle. Is it your death the white tiger prophesied, or another's?"

"Another's. The death of my partner, Charles Ramh. He is to be struck down by the outraged temple gods."

Seekay showed no surprise at all. He only nodded, with dim light streaks reflecting from his inhuman shield.

"I see. And why is he to be stricken?"

"Because of the white tiger," said the East Indian. "The tiger guarded the temple in India. We had it killed and brought here to sell it, mounted, because of its rarity. The gods, angry because the temple is now unguarded, mean to strike us dead. My partner, Ramh, was warned first. That was this morning at ten, two hours ago."

"Have you been to the police at all?"

The East Indian shook his head. "The police force of Chicago would hardly interest itself in a warning from a dead tiger. But I thought you might."

"What business are you and your partner in? Importing?"

"Yes. There are three of us. Ramh, Lakhdar, and myself. My name is Lall. We import rugs, leather work, brasses, jade—all the Indian art work—and sell it here in the Middle West of the United States. Now and then we get rarities like the White Tiger—which I wish we had never heard of."

"Tell me about the warning."

"It was at our apartment. Ramh and I have a floor on Lincoln Park. The white tiger stands in a glass case at the rear of our living-room. Around it are other cases containing goods for sale and some valuable pieces which are our own. I was at a desk in the front of the room by the boulevard windows. My partner was at the rear near the case. I heard a voice. It was a whispering, sibilant voice, like the hiss of a great cat. It said, 'You are to die. The white tiger has spoken.'

"My partner said the voice was addressed to him, and that it came from the opened jaws of the tiger. We talked, wondering what to do. We do not believe in the old gods of India. And yet.... The Tiger had been the guardian of a temple north of Calcutta. By our orders it had been trapped, and killed when it was found impossible to ship it out alive, which left the temple without its guard."

Lall drew a deep breath. "We talked it over. While we were discussing it, almost deciding our ears had played us tricks, the tiger spoke again. And again it said the same thing. So then I said I would come to you."

"And your partner?"

"He is at the apartment, with a gun in his hand. The gun is aimed at the tiger in the glass case. We do not believe in the old gods, but.... He is watching it for his life!"

Seekay almost overturned his chair in his haste to rise.

Marian stared at him in amazement and a growing apprehension born of his unusual impulsiveness. Seekay was not an impulsive man.

"You say the tiger case is at the rear of the room?"

"Yes."

"And you left your partner, Ramh, with a gun leveled at it."

"Yes, but—"

"Come along. At once. My car, Miss Ford, as fast as it can be rolled from the garage. I think we are already too late. But there may be a chance—"

SEEKAY'S POWERFUL coupe stopped before a tall apartment building on Chicago's Lincoln Park. He got out of the car with Marian close behind him, and the Indian following. He hurried into the lobby and into an automatic elevator. Lall pressed the tenth-floor button, and the cage shot upward.

"You think…" faltered Lall, face more greenish than ever.

"I think that to remain motionless with a gun pointed at a stuffed tiger in a glass case may be the deadliest thing a man can do," snapped Seekay. "But we'll soon see. This is the door? Open it."

The elevator had opened onto a tiny foyer with one locked door on it. Lall opened the door and the three stepped into the huge living-room of the sumptuous apartment that took up the entire tenth floor of the building.

And then Marian screamed softly. For with the opening of the door it was revealed to them that they were too late. The white tiger had spoken truly.

The big living-room looked like a museum. It was lined with glass cases containing semi-precious gems, specimens of rare jades, and East Indian metal work. At the far end of the chamber was a bigger case than any of the others. In this was a tiger, a giant of his kind—a brute that was greyish white, instead of tawny and striped as it should have been. It stood in the case, in a remarkably lifelike way, with jaws open and snarling, glassy eyes glaring at the three.

And before it on the floor, with face up as though staring into the tiger's snarling jaws, lay a dead man.

A bleating cry of fear came from Lall's lips. He darted forward, with Seekay beside him.

RAMH WAS dead enough. It took little examination to substantiate that. His face was mottled grey, his eyes were closed, his hands had the extreme limpness of death, before rigor mortis has set in. There was horror on his face, and he lay with his head tilted as though even in death he listened fearfully to impossible warnings from a fantastic source.

Seekay straightened up. He stared at the glass case, slowly walked around it. Marian's gaze followed him. She was shuddering a little. Had this dead, stuffed beast actually killed a man? She thought she knew for what Seekay might be hunting: bullet holes in the glass case—perhaps made by bullets coming from *inside* it. Or possibly he was searching for signs that the glass lid or side had recently been removed....

Almost indifferently, Seekay left the case and stepped to the dead man again. He sank to his knees beside him. Overcoming her fear and repugnance, Marian came closer. She watched as Seekay made swift examination of the body. She saw what Seekay had seen: There was not a mark on the dead man—nothing to indicate the manner of his death.

Seekay, with Lall wandering around the room like a man who does not know what he is doing, picked up the dead man's hands. Minutely, he scrutinized the fingernails, slightly purplish at their bases. Then he did something rather ghastly.

He turned to the face, and his long-fingered hands went out. His thumbs pressed lightly at the corners of the closed eyelids. They opened a little, revealing staring eyeballs. He pressed a little harder with his thumbs, and Marian bit back an exclamation.

The dead eyes seemed to roll a bit and then to stare straight up into Seekay's glittering black eyes. The faceless detective held them that way for a long time, and meanwhile stared intently into the eyes. Was he reading dread things there in some uncanny way, Marian wondered? Did the dead eyes have some last imprinted message to give him—

Lall exclaimed aloud suddenly, and ran toward the alcove of the room, in front. Seekay and Marian turned. They saw him leap behind the desk there, and then back out of it dragging another body.

"It is our servant, Shimshe. Dead, too!"

But the man, slight, scholarly looking, not wearing a turban as was Lall, and such as appeared on Ramh's head, was not dead. As Lall lowered him to the floor again after dragging him out from behind the desk, he moaned and stirred.

"O, Tiger, spare me...."

Suddenly, he began struggling wildly against Lall's touch. He sat up, glaring around, with the frenzy subsiding only a little in his eyes as he saw those around him.

"The tiger! It struck! Beware—"

He fainted again. Seekay's black eyes raked his still face, then the faceless detective walked back to Ramh's body. Again he opened the dead eyes and stared long and tensely at the eyeballs which had rolled a little at the touch of his thumbs.

"All right," he said to Marian. "Call the police."

He turned to Lall. "This other partner of yours, Lakhdar, does not live here?"

"No. He has a house to the north, in a ways from the lake."

"Lakhdar is not an Indian name."

"It is Arab," said Lall. "He was in business in Tunis, before he joined our partnership."

The man's face was yellowish-green, now. "I—I might be suspected of this death of my partner?"

"Suspected?" said Seekay. "You'll be charged definitely with it, and held for trial. The address of Lakhdar's house? Thank you. I may be back here before the police take you away."

He stared at the white tiger. Its glassy eyes glared and its snarling jaws seemed to open more widely. From those jaws, it was said, a death threat had come, and now a dead man lay at the white tiger's feet. The gods of India had spoken—and acted.

CHAPTER TWO
BULLET OF GREAT PRICE

SEEKAY WHIRLED the big coupe toward the address given by Lall. Marian watched him out of the corners of her deep blue eyes.

She stood in awe of the incisive, mysterious detective, seldom speaking when he was working on one of his bizarre cases unless he spoke to her first.

His hands turned the coupe's wheel deftly. She liked his hands, square, powerful, long-fingered. She liked the dark, thick hair over his mask. She stared, baffled, at the street mask he wore, with a gentle smile painted on its waxen lips—a smile that was horrible sometimes when his eyes burned death for some opponent. His eyes could change expression; the painted lips could not.

She couldn't control her curiosity any longer.

"What killed Ramh? Do you know?"

"I think I do," said Seekay calmly. "And I think I know who it was. But there must be proof."

"Who?" demanded Marian excitedly.

"The white tiger, guardian of the violated Indian temple."

Marian relaxed in disappointment. "You don't believe that stuff."

"But I do," said Seekay.

"How could a thing in a glass case kill a man?"

Seekay was silent, guiding the coupe at fifty miles an hour along a street where fifteen would have been risky.

"Here's our place," he said, finally, "A luxurious-looking house. There must be money in the Indian importing business. You can stay out in the car if you like. It will be bad inside."

"You think Lakhdar is in danger?"

"I think he is dead," said Seekay. "If he isn't, then he will be soon. Two of the partners must die."

"Why are you so sure? And why two?"

"Because," said Seekay, "there are two eyes in even an idol's head."

And with that he rang the bell at the front door of the red brick house in front of which they had stopped. There was no answer. He got out a flat leather case and calmly picked the lock. Marian stayed with him as he entered the house. She preferred being with him to staying out in the car alone.

She had several times thought that her senses had become abnormally acute since she had started to work for the private operative who baffled the police as well as the public with his uncanny ability. She had reason to think that again, now. For she felt, as they stepped into the front hall and Seekay closed the door behind them, that something was hideously wrong in this place.

Seekay led the way, as surely as though he had been in the house before, to a door at the right of the hail. It was a double sliding-door, closed. He drew the big portals back. And for the second time within the hour Marian bit back a scream as she gazed on death.

A TALL, dark, emaciated man lay on the floor near the doorway. He lay half on his face, as though listening to some faint, far sound. His eyes were opened, and the expression on his face was one of agony and horror. He had been wearing an Oriental headdress of the Arabic type—a fez wound around with a turban strip. It had slipped from his close-cropped hair, leaving his head bare.

Seekay bent over the body, eyes blazing, but cold mask gently smiling as its painted lips must always smile no matter what the occasion. Again he examined a body for marks. And again Marian saw, with him, that not one mark showed. Not the slightest sign of a wound, or even of a scratch where poison might have entered the fortress of the skin.

Not one mark on him—but he was dead with a look of abysmal horror on his face!

"So the white tiger spoke twice," Seekay said softly. "Once to Ramh, once to Lakhdar. And both Ramh and Lakhdar are now dead."

He looked at this dead man's eyes as he had at the other's. With his thumbs he pressed at the corners of the lids till they opened wider. Then he pressed a bit harder till the glazing eyeballs rolled and seemed to peer directly into his own black eyes. Intently, bent far down, he stared into the dead pupils.

"What—do you see there?" said Marian shakily. "Why do you look so hard into dead men's eyes? And why, out in the car, did you make the remark that there are two eyes even in an idol's head?"

Seekay did not answer. The answer was circumvented before it could possibly come from his masked lips. And it was almost circumvented by death.

There was a soft hissing sound. Marian heard something whisper past her ear, and then saw plaster fly from a spot in the near wall almost on a line with Seekay's head. A bullet, noiselessly cleaving the air for his skull! And it would have found its mark if Seekay hadn't chanced to move his head down nearer yet to the dead man's eyes a fraction of a second before the silent bullet was fired.

Seekay was on his feet and leaping for the window before an ordinary man could have recovered movement at all from the deadly surprise. The window was open six inches at the top. He hauled down hard on it. But it was held fast at the six inch mark by a burglar catch. He crashed his fist through the glass and leaned out.

Across a narrow alley and to the right was a low garage roof. As he stared, something whitish loped over the far edge of the roof and out of sight. The mysterious attacker had escaped. Seekay turned back.

Marian had gone, white-faced, to the wall where the bullet had hit. There was not a very large nor deep hole in the plaster. The bullet lay on the floor beneath. She picked it up. Seekay, coming toward her, heard her gasp. His black eyes stared a question through the eyeholes of the painted face he wore.

"Look! It's a diamond! At least it looks like one."

Seekay took the "bullet" she held toward him. Enigmatically, he examined it.

It was a thing as big as a robin's egg, rather crudely faceted but sparkling with the fires of hell in spite of its crude and ancient-seeming cut. If it was a diamond it was a huge and valuable one—too valuable, it would seem, to

be propelled at a man's head in place of an ordinary, valueless lead slug.

Seekay nodded and slipped the thing into his pocket.

"Well, I guess this tells the rest of the story. We have it
all, now. And it also tells that you and I walk with our lives
held lightly in our hands, ready to drop, till I catch the
white tiger. There is death in my pocket with this thing."

He started back toward the door, then stopped with a
jerk. Marian saw his eyes flame at something on the floor,
and turned to look, too. Her blood chilled at what she saw.

On a section of the parquet floor not covered by valuable
oriental rugs, there was a single faint mark. A sort of great
seal set in the slight dust that had settled there. An enormous seal, and a fantastic one.

There, on the bare boards, was the single print of a huge
tiger.

IT WAS about three in the afternoon when Seekay and
Marian got back to the apartment of Lall and the deceased
Lakhdar. The place swarmed with the police, and the body
still had not been moved. The reason for the slowness came
out as they were faced by Ackley, city detective who knew
Seekay, grudgingly respected his ability, sneered at him
whenever there was any one to listen, and took the credit
for the private detective's work whenever possible.

"What do you know about this?" he demanded bluntly,
as Seekay came in carrying a black box about the size of
a large camera. His voice was heavy to match his body,
and, sometimes, his wits.

"What have you found out?" Seekay countered, with
the mask over his face baffling the city detective as it baffled
all who would read his thoughts.

Ackley tilted his hat back on his head. "Not much. It looks like murder because those two brown guys, Shimshe and Lall, were gone when we got here. Tryin' to make a getaway. We caught Lall at the Northwestern Station, and Shimshe at the next corner. They said they were beating it because they figured the white tiger would get them next if they stuck around."

Ackley snorted, and stared at the big glass case in which the pale tiger snarled eternally with open jaws and glared with glassy eyes.

"The crust! Saying a tiger in a glass case killed this guy, and that it'd kill them next if they didn't beat it! We left everything as it was and dragged 'em back here to grill 'em right on the murder scene. Neither knuckled-under. Maybe they will in a headquarters back room."

"I doubt that," said Seekay. "So you've proved it was murder?"

Ackley stared suspiciously at the black eyes showing in the mask's eyeholes. Then he scratched his head.

"Well, no, we haven't. There ain't a mark on Ramh's body anywhere. But maybe he was gassed or poisoned. Autopsy will show that. The coroner's been here so we'll ship the stiff to the morgue—"

"After I've had a moment with it," Seekay said incisively. "Where are Lall and Shimshe?"

"Locked up in a room back there." The detective jerked his head toward the rear of the apartment. "Want to see them?"

Seekay nodded, and walked toward the back. Ackley stuck close. He never let the faceless detective out of his sight on a case if he could help it. There was too much probability that Seekay would turn up something Ackley wouldn't.

Seekay talked to Lall first.

"Why did you try to get away? You must have known it would look suspicious."

Lall stared into the black eyes. He was controlling his terror less effectively now. His face was grey, and beads of perspiration showed on it. He muttered a few phrases in his own tongue.

"I was not getting away from the police," he said, after a moment. "I was fleeing from the white tiger."

"From a stuffed animal mounted in a glass case?"

"From the white tiger," Lall repeated stubbornly. "I do not want to die. And unless I can get far away and hide, I am going to die. I know that now, after what Shimshe told me."

"What did he tell you?"

"He told me how the white tiger struck."

"When?"

"After you had gone, before the police came."

"What did he tell you?"

Lall's lips closed with hysterical stubbornness.

SEEKAY WASTED no more time on him. He knew when a man was through talking. He went to Shimshe, locked in the next room. "Lall says you saw the white tiger strike. How was it done?"

It looked for a moment as though Shimshe would not talk, either. But finally his lips moved. The slender little man was more nervy than Lall. His eyes showed equal terror, but his face and body were composed.

"I did not see it strike," he said, in scholarly English. "But I saw my master, Ramh, fall." He leaned slightly forward.

"Well?"

"I was beside him when my master, Lall, left to go to you. I, too, stood watch over the white tiger, but not with a gun in my hand. For I knew, if my master, Ramh, did not, that no gun would save one from the wrath of the white guardian of the despoiled temple. I was staring at the tiger when I saw its eyes seem to grow. They became larger and larger. I stared hypnotized. So, too, I think, did my master, Ramh. At least he was motionless beside me. The eyes grew so large that we seemed about to fall into them. A voice came from the case: 'You, who ordered the death of the white temple guardian, now shall die yourself.' And with that, my master, Ramh, fell to the floor."

Ackley snorted loudly. Marian looked from the earnest; terrified face of Shimshe to the painted face-mask of Seekay.

"What's a guy supposed to do with a yarn like that?" Ackley sneered.

Seekay didn't look at him. His black eyes continued on the Indian servant's face. "You think Ramh was struck down by the spirit of the white tiger?"

The man nodded. "By the white tiger. Or by the gods on high. It does not matter which. He is dead. And I, too, will die if I cannot flee far and fast and find a deep and secret hiding place."

It was an echo of Lall's frantic words. Seekay went back to Lall's prison-room. "What disposal is to be made of Ramh's body?" he asked.

"It will go back to his native land," Lall replied. "Mine, too, is to be shipped back to India when I die."

"To be placed in a Tower of Silence for the vultures to pick the bones clean?"

"No," said Lall. "I am not of that religious sect, nor was Ramh."

"And Lakhdar?" said Seekay quietly.

Lall shrieked, "Lakhdar?"

"He is dead. And near him on the floor there is a single great tiger print."

Ackley jumped forward. "Hey! You mean this guy's other partner? He was knocked off, too? Why the hell didn't you tell me? How do you get that way, letting a murder lie around for a couple hours—"

"Some of your buddies on the homicide squad are over there," Seekay said indifferently.

"Leave me out of here! I'm going over there and look around. And if a tiger of any color killed Lakhdar, or Ramh, I'll find 'im and put cuffs on his paws!" He brandished his big fists.

But for a moment more Ackley did not leave. Seekay had said he wanted one more moment with Ramh's corpse, and the city detective wanted to know what for. He stayed with Seekay as the private detective walked back to the body lying before the glass case.

Seekay took the black box he carried and opened a shallow tray in its lid. From this he took a coil of electric wire, which he hooked into the nearest baseboard. Then he bent over the corpse and pointed the box at the dead man's eyes. In a way, he aimed it, for all the world as if he were using a camera, photographing the corpse's eyeballs.

Ackley writhed with curiosity, finally couldn't contain it any longer.

"What're you doing?"

"Reading the record of a dead man's eyes," said Seekay. "Dead eyes can tell tales, Ackley."

Marian, listening, knew how the city detective felt. She had been evaded often enough herself by Seekay when she asked about his methods and discoveries before he felt like talking about them.

"I heard a guy say once that the last thing a man looked at before he died was set in the retina of his eye, like a picture on a photographic plate," Ackley said, clearing his throat. "Is that straight? And are you taking a picture of a picture on Ramh's retina?"

"I'm taking a picture," shrugged Seekay. "I think I know what it will reveal. Tell you when I've developed it...."

He left the apartment, with Ackley at his heels. At the street door the city detective, fuming, left for the house of Lakhdar, while Seekay went to his own home, and to his laboratory.

A little later he was in his private office, with his more comfortable pink celluloid shield in place over his features. What features? Marian asked the question inwardly as she had a thousand times. Why did Seekay cover his face with the hideous blank shield in his home, and with the painted face-mask when he walked abroad? For what mysterious, possibly horrible, reason couldn't his real face be exposed to the world?

Seekay tossed over a still-wet sheet of paper. A newly developed print showing an X-ray picture, taken by the black box, which was in reality a small, marvelously efficient X-ray machine of his own devising, with tiny camera attachment.

The print showed a man's head. Ramh's, taken from the front at about eye level. The bone of the skull showed shadowy. The brain tissue had faded out. But right behind the ghostly left eye-socket there was a hard bold black object. And Marian felt a finger of ice creep up her back as she looked at it.

No mistaking it. The clarity with which it showed left nothing uncertain. All its crude facets and ancient style of cutting were revealed. The hard black little object embedded in the dead man's brain was a diamond.

"He was killed as you were almost killed at Lakhdar's house!" Marian exclaimed. "By a diamond bullet!"

Seekay said nothing. And, staring into his black eyes, Marian remembered something. There had been no sign of any bullet hole in the dead man's skull.

Face and head had been unmarked—yet there, buried deeply in the brain tissue, was the diamond bullet.

"It's black magic," whispered Marian.

"You can't shoot a diamond bullet into a man's skull without leaving a hole."

Seekay shrugged. "A stuffed animal in a glass case can't kill, either. Yet the white tiger did this."

"Was Lakhdar killed by a diamond bullet?"

"We'll see," said Seekay. "You know how to use my X-ray box. Take it, and go to Lakhdar's house. The body will still be there. X-ray his head. That is, if you will undertake so distasteful a job?"

"I'm under orders," said Marian steadily. "I knew when I went to work for you that it wouldn't be like working in a flower shop."

"Good girl," said Seekay. "Here, take this diamond bullet that we got at Lakhdar's. Give it to Ackley." He took the big stone from his pocket and handed it to her. "Be careful of it. And—watch out for the white tiger."

Marian took the black box and the diamond and went to the door. She threw it wide and started to leave, their stopped in her tracks and stared at the hall floor.

There, just the other side of the door that had been closed on Seekay and her, was the dusty print of a great paw.

She looked at Seekay. His keen eyes had caught it too. They swung to her blue ones.

"As I said, Miss Ford—*watch out for the tiger!*"

She straightened her shoulders and went out.

Seekay went back to his desk and picked up his phone. He dialed the Carson Museum, and got hold of the Indian curator there.

"North of Calcutta," he said, "there is a temple held by a little-known sect called the Devotees of the White Tiger. They consist of a high priest and perhaps a dozen minor priests. The temple is guarded—or was guarded—by a great white tiger. Is that right?"

"That's right," came the voice of the curator.

"Thank you. I wanted to refresh my memory. Tell me, would Carson Museum be interested in having that white tiger, expertly mounted, for its animal collection?"

"It certainly would."

"How much would it pay?"

Well, not a fortune. But a large sum."

"It has not been offered to you for sale?"

"It has not."

"Thank you," said Seekay. "Good-by."

"Wait! Who is this calling—?"

Seekay hung up, black eyes glittering more brightly, fingers tensing in a sort of clawing motion on his desk.

CHAPTER THREE
WHAT THE DEAD SEE

MARIAN PRESSED the bell at Lakhdar's house again. She had rung once, clearly, and no answering buzzer noise had sounded.

It seemed odd, with all the police there must be in the place, that no one would hear. It was also odd that she saw no squad car in front of the house.

The buzzer sounded at last. She opened the door and stepped into a quiet hall. The black box was in her right hand. With the fingers of her left, she felt instinctively at her waist. There, in a secret pocket in her girdle, lay the great diamond, with its fires seeming to burn into her flesh.

Still she heard no sound in the house. The silence, where she had expected buzzing activity, rasped her nerves like a file. She half-turned to go back out, then shrugged and walked down the hall toward the death room.

The door of the room was closed. She slid it back, as Seekay had done when they first came here. And she stepped into a room not disturbed much from its condition when she and Seekay had first seen it. There were traces of powder on chairbacks, phone, and knobs, where print men had searched for fingerprints. But the body still lay as it had. She started toward it. Ackley and the rest must be on an upper floor....

The breath was forced between her white, even teeth in an audible gasp. There was a heavy drape beside the street window. It hung to the floor. But at the floor it bulged out a little—and she could see the square tip of one capacious shoe.

She screamed softly, and darted forward. Her hand swept back the drape.

Another dead man lay there. This was a patrolman in uniform. He lay on his back, dead eyes staring widely up at her. His head had been crushed by a tremendous blow, and from the edges of the wound a little blood still trickled. Marian backed away to run. The man had been dead only a few minutes. So short a time that it seemed whatever had killed him must be still in the house—

"Stand where you are. Don't move."

The voice came from behind her. And never had she heard anything like it. The tone was not human. It was that of a snarling beast. The words had been hissed out, as a great cat might hiss them.

"You—you are the white tiger?" she heard the words and hardly realized that they had come from her lips.

"I am the white tiger. Guardian of the despoiled temple. *Stand still*—"

But the words were too late. Marian had turned. Not for life itself could she have kept her body from making that convulsive move. She couldn't stand with her back to this thing. The horror of not knowing what was behind her was worse than knowing—and dying.

She screamed again, wildly, as her eyes came to rest on a great figure that was whitish-grey, half-crouching, snarling with rigid jaws. Then she was beyond screaming as her eyes told the rest of the tale.

THE SNARLING head of the figure was that of a white tiger. But the rest of the body seemed to be that of a man, clad in whitish-grey. The hands were those of a man. Those hands were held a little ahead of the bizarre figure. The left was empty, with clawing, talon fingers. The right held a slender ivory scepter, in the top of which was set a glittering crystal ball. Her eyes were riveted by its sparkle.

"You have the diamond bullet." The words hissed through snarling jaws.

The crystal ball was growing in size. It seemed a foot in diameter now, where at first it had been only three or four inches. And as it grew, its glitter increased, dazzling her, blinding her.

"I have the diamond bullet," she heard herself reply, in a dazed, mechanical voice.

"Give it to me."

But in Marian there was a sudden dim rebellion at that. Somewhere in her brain was a slight corner not yet blinded by the crystal.

"Give it to me!"

Her hands writhed by her sides—but stayed there.

"You are not going to live, anyway. Those who have seen the tiger, die—and you have seen the tiger. You may as well give up the diamond."

The hissing words, for all their deadly content, seemed almost soothing. Marian reeled a little, felt like sinking to the floor.... The crystal ball was a crystal world, folding over her.... She felt it touch her.

No, the touch was that of talon fingers, going over her body slowly, inch by inch, stopping at last at her waist. Fingers searching.... Ah, yes, for the diamond bullet! And then the fingers moved again.

Marian was hardly conscious any more. She only knew that she still stood unsteadily there, and that the fingers were twisting at the fastenings of her dress. The dress was slid down over her hips to the floor. Her slip followed. The fingers ripped at the slender girdle from which her garters hung, and then its pressure was gone from her waist. Her body felt cold in the cool room. She was, she realized, naked save for stockings and sheer brassiere, but the realization was dim and inconsequential beside the feeling of sick horror that held her in the dim captivity of her trance.

"Those who have seen the tiger, die. And you have seen the tiger."

The death sentence tore at her soul. But she could not move. She could only stand there, a living statue, with the dead policeman and the dead Lakhdar beside her.

The compelling glitter of the crystal receded a little, and, as though through a mist, she could see the figure with the man's body and the beast's head. In its hand was the diamond with the ancient cut. The hand went down toward the dead Lakhdar's face....

Marian thought she screamed, then. Actually no sound passed her rigid lips. But she thought she shrieked again and again at the thing transpiring before her eyes.

The thumb of the *thing's* right hand was pressing at the dead man's left eye. Harder it pressed, with the eyelids straining open more widely, till finally the eyeball moved sideways in its socket. And then it left the socket altogether. In its place, the ruthless hand set the diamond, to sparkle there in its fleshly setting like the crystalized eye of a fiend.

The bizarre figure with the body of a human and the head of an animal bent lower over the dead man's face. Its shoulders gathered a little, then became rigid.

The doorway of the room was shadowed for an instant as a figure slid softly in.

By a great effort, Marian forced her eyes from the grisly spectacle to her right, and stared ahead at the doorway. The face she saw sent a wild shock of hope lancing through the coma that had seized her. It was the painted mask of Seekay.

HE STOOD just inside the doorway, black eyes burning at the crouching, fantastic figure. His eyes flicked to her, at the silken little heap of her clothing on the floor, then back to the thing bending over Lakhdar's corpse. The thing with the bestial head had made one quick downward move. The diamond no longer sparkled evilly in the dead man's eyesocket. The eye was there instead. Long fingers smoothed the lid down over it....

"Better than a jewel casket, isn't it?" came Seekay's deep, level voice.

The figure with the tiger head screamed and whirled. Then, in spite of the gun held in Seekay's right hand, the thing started a slow, deadly advance toward him, crouching, with the scepter advanced and the crystal sparkling.

"I'm afraid you can't hypnotize me as you hypnotized my assistant," Seekay said. "And I know this gun holds no threat for you because you do not fear death. But you had better stop where you are."

The fantastic figure had now advanced to within leaping distance.

"If you don't stop," said Seekay, "those diamonds will never reach India."

It was a meaningless sentence to Marian, but it seemed to have tremendous significance to the creature. For it stopped, a hiss coming from the snarling jaws.

"That's better," Seekay said evenly. "Now I'll strike a bargain with you. I am not entirely lacking in sympathy for your cause, but there are three dead men to be accounted for. If you will write down a confession of murder, I will let you die by your own hand—and I will say nothing about the diamonds."

The figure trembled there, on the verge of completing a desperate leap in spite of the gun, but not quite taking the plunge.

"There is a desk to your right," Seekay said. "On it is a pen. There will be paper in one of the drawers."

The bizarre figure went to the desk. Marian's throat trembled with a hysterical desire to laugh. Seated—a human body with the head of a tiger....

But the figure made no move to pick up the pen. Words hissed from its jaws.

"You can prove nothing, actually."

SEEKAY'S SHOULDERS moved. "I'll dictate the whole thing, if you like. It starts with the temple of the White Tiger, north of Calcutta, and with a high priest and an idol and a huge white tiger that roamed loose in the temple grounds as guard. The temple had been inviolate for centuries. Then despoilers who did not believe in the old gods killed the tiger, entered the temple and looted it. Tiger and loot came into the hands of Ramh, Lall and Lakhdar. The high priest followed vengefully after.

"This morning a voice came from the dead thing in the glass case. It was not difficult. One of a high priest's lesser abilities must be that of ventriloquism, so that words may seem to come from an idol's lips. The white tiger decreed death to Ramh. Lall came to me, seeking protection, and said their crime had been only to take the white tiger from the temple to sell its rare skin here. But that was proved to be a lie—the Carson Museum, here, said the animal had never been—offered to them for sale, though they are the likeliest market. So there was something more. What? Jewels. From the idol's eyes—for that was the custom in old India.

"I went with Lall and found Ramh dead. While he had foolishly faced the glass case containing the tiger, death had stolen up behind him. Death in the form of a poisoned needle thrust suddenly under his thumb-nail. I saw that Ramh's eyes were closed. But a man's eyes are usually open in death, unless a hand has closed them afterward. I examined to see why. they were closed, and found that the left eyeball moved too easily in its socket. It had been removed and then replaced after something had been forced through the thin bony plate at the rear of the socket into the skull so no outer marks would show. What had been thrust into the concealing brain? One of the temple jewels—one of the idol's eyes, of course.

"It was pretty plain, then. The body of Ramh was to be sent home to India. It would go bearing one of the sacred gems torn from the idol's eye-socket at his orders, and be retrieved from his skull by the priests of the White Tiger on its arrival. Safe passage for the jewel, poetic justice in that it was forced into the fleshly socket of the man by whose order it had been taken from a stone socket.

"But there were two gems—two eyes of the idol. So another must die to provide safe and secret passage back to the Orient. Revenge would not be enough if only one died and was shipped back with both gems in his brain. So death struck at Lakhdar. But I got to his body before the stone could be forced through the socket. You were at the window, where you had retreated with our entrance. You had a powerful sling in your pocket but no stone missile. However, you had the big diamond, as good as any other projectile. You shot it at me, intending to stun me, enter and kill us both, and go on with your work. But the diamond missed, leaving you with the task of retrieving it once more.

"You allowed yourself to be caught by the police and taken back to Ramh's apartment. There you would probably see me again and learn my plans, and my movements were now your sole concern. You saw me X-ray Ramh's skull, knew your plan was discovered, and followed me back to my home, after escaping by hypnotizing your police guard. There you overheard my assistant and me in my office, heard me send her here with the diamond. Oh, I knew you were outside the door, my friend. Photo-electric cells and black rays do not lie. They tell the truth when a trespasser enters their sphere, and tell where the trespasser is. I wanted you to hear, for I was regretfully setting a trap for you with my assistant as bait.

"And you entered the trap. You came here, after drawing the men of the homicide squad away from the house, killed the man they left on guard, and waited for my assistant and the diamond. You were about through with your task, ready to kill her, and me later, and return to your native land and your temple, with the idol's eyes following in two dead men's brains and your revenge accomplished."

SEEKAY'S VOICE died. The silence in the room was deathly. The figure at the desk sat with bestial head bowed down. Its arms hung down below the edge of the desk. Marian could see the arms from where she stood, and the wrists and hands. She tried to scream aloud as horror swamped her soul, and still she could not, nor could she move. Words came from the figure, thick and uncertain.

"If I confess to all this, you will allow the diamonds to go back to where they belong in the skulls of these blasphemers?"

"I will," said Seekay. "No one knows of them and their hiding place but me. I will say nothing. You are a murderer, but you murdered through religious conviction. As high priest, you really believe that in you dwells the soul of the Tiger guardian and avenger."

"You even know that I am—Shimshe?" came the hissing voice, more weakly still.

"Of course. It was made pretty plain when I went with Lall to the apartment and found Ramh dead and you supposedly unconscious. But when you pretended recovery from unconsciousness, you spoke careful English. No man would speak an alien tongue on such recovery. He would leave unconsciousness with words of his native language coming dazedly from his lips. I knew pretty surely who was guilty, then, but there was no proof."

"And there will be no proof now, with your death!" came screaming from the tiger's head.

With the first word, the figure had leaped up. Its hand flashed forward, throwing the keen blade Marian had seen slide slowly from coat sleeve into waiting fingers. The glittering blade sped true to Seekay's heart. But it thudded harmlessly against his coat, and fell to the floor.

"Bullet-proof vest, Shimshe," said Seekay. "Also knife proof." And he fired, unemotionally, once.

The clock struck four-thirty as the echo of the barking shot died down.

The fantastic figure fell, with the tiger head rolling from its shoulders as it sagged, to reveal the thin, scholarly features of Shimshe. Also with it fell a sort of glove, padded to resemble a tiger's paw, with which the seal of the White Tiger had been made.

CHAPTER FOUR
THE GRAVE
KEEPS ITS SECRET

MARIAN HAD her clothes on. Seekay's hands, clapped sharply before her face, had roused her at last from the stupor into which Shimshe had plunged her. There was a crash at the street door, and the sound of men bursting angrily in. They stood at the door, three of them, with Ackley at their head. His face was purple.

"You, Seekay! Was it your phony call that Lall had just been murdered back at his joint that got us all out of here?"

"So that's how he worked it?" Seekay said. Then, "No. It wasn't I who wanted this house cleared. It was this man, Shimshe." He pointed to the dead man in the greyish linen suit. "He's your killer, Ackley. You'll find the pad he made the sign of the tiger with, and plenty of other things to prove him guilty. Also a dead patrolman there, killed by him."

Ackley swore softly. "Dolan! I left him here on guard when we beat it back to Lall's on the fake phone call. And then we found Lall okay, and Shimshe gone, and the cop who was guarding Shimshe kind of asleep on his feet. And we couldn't snap him out of it. He stayed that way till a kind of funny thing happened. At half-past four, just before we beat it back here, the damn white tiger fell over on its side in the glass case. Nobody was anywhere near it. It just fell over, for no reason. And then Shimshe's guard came out of his dopey dreams."

Marian's eyes sought Seekay's. *At four-thirty the white tiger had fallen over on its side.*

At four-thirty, Shimshe, head of the cult of the White Tiger and firmly believing the tiger's soul dwelt in his body, had fallen over on *his* side with Seekay's bullet through his heart!

Ackley glared at Seekay. "What else did you find out here?"

"Nothing more," said Seekay steadily. He spoke no word of the diamonds.

"Let them go back to the temple where they belong," he said to Marian in the big coupe as they rolled toward his home. "Shimshe gave his life to that end, and it's no more than Rahm and Lakhdar deserve. Lall's lucky to be alive."

Marian said nothing. She was remembering her state as Seekay came into the room, the minutes she had stood in the hypnotic spell clad only in brassiere and shoes and stockings. She glanced sideways at Seekay. His eyes met hers.

"You have a right to be angry at me for sending you back there deliberately as bait, when I knew an attack might be made on your life. I wouldn't blame you for quitting your job."

"I'm—not quitting," said Marian.

Seekay's painted mask of a face turned toward the street and his driving again. But his big hand rested on hers.

"I'm glad, Marian." Then his voice became almost light as he said, "May the blessings of the White Tiger be on us as we pursue our work—together."

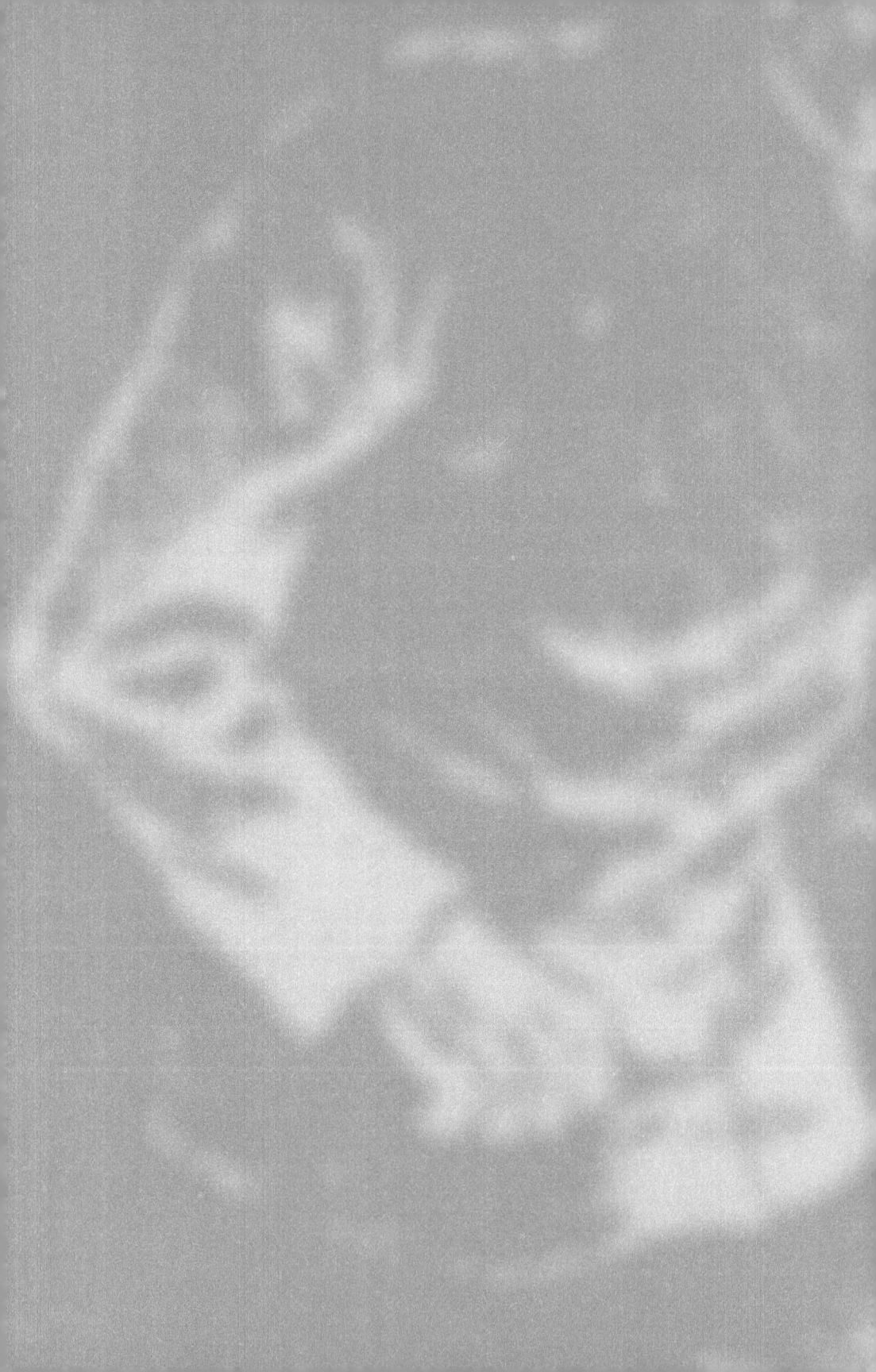

CASE OF THE SMOKING SKULLS

WHOSE HAND SMOTHERED HELEN FREEL'S SCREAM IN THE DEPARTING TAXI? AND HOW HAD DEATH COME TO THE MAN LYING ON THE SIDEWALK? WHAT EERIE MENACE CENTERED IN THE OLD MILLIONAIRE'S FORTRESS-LIKE HOUSE? THE PAINTED SMILE ON SEEKAY'S MASK REMAINED UNCHANGED AS HE FOLLOWED STEP BY STEP THE TRAIL OF THE MYSTERIOUS KILLER.

CHAPTER ONE
DEATH COMES VISITING

ONE DIM light was all that illuminated the big room, though it was heavily shaded from the dusk outside. But then the huge office was usually kept in darkness because of Seekay's face. Or, rather, his lack of a face.

Abandoning for the moment her position by the tall window, Marian Ford glanced toward the big desk behind which her employer sat. The eccentric private detective was leaning back in his swivel chair—a tall, powerful body in brown tweeds, his muscular hands lightly clasped together. He was as silent and impassive as the mask over his face.

Marian stared at that mask. It was a half-cylinder of pinkish, celluloid-like material; a shield that covered his countenance from below his chin to the line of black hair, streaked with gray, at his forehead.

What was under that grim, smooth surface, through openings in which Seekay's eyes, now closed in apparent sleep, usually appeared as blazing bits of jet? Even Marian, his own secretary, didn't know. Perhaps there was some monstrous deformation of his real features; some hideous birthmark or burn that he was trying to hide from the world....

"The street, please, Marian," Seekay said suddenly, his deep organ-like voice smooth.

Marian gasped a little. She could see the closed lids of Seekay's eyes through the eyeholes of his shield. How could he tell that she was staring at him instead of out into the street? But she didn't ask. Probably some slight stir of the fabric of her dress had sounded when she turned her head from the window to desk, and his phenomenally keen ears had picked it up.

She read death in the maniac's eyes.

"She should have been here by now," Seekay said, his tones betraying an impatience foreign to his usual phlegmatic character.

"It's a woman's privilege to be late, as well as to change her mind," Marian murmured as she stared through a small clear circle in the otherwise heavily stained front windows of Seekay's office.

"She will not change her mind about seeing me," Seekay said positively. "It is amazing enough that she is late. Her voice when she phoned to make the appointment a half-hour ago.... I have never heard more terror. She was obvi-

ously fearful that she was being followed." He paused a moment and then said slowly, as if to himself: "No, she will come—if she can. Devil-ridden, that's what she was. Devil-ridden...."

MARIAN MADE no comment. Most of Seekay's clients were "devil-ridden"—people driven in the last extremity of fear and horror to seek the help of the man to whom they turned only when the regular police could do nothing for them.

Outside, it was a clear, cool, early spring night. March in Chicago can be a crisp delight, in its rare moments. This was one of the rare ones: the sky a royal canopy of deep velvet, studded with millions of twinkling diamonds, the air tangy and dry.

A delivery truck rattled through the quiet street, past the tall, inconspicuous house which Seekay owned and used as both home and office. It was followed by a town car, moving with silence and majesty. A cab came from the opposite direction.

"And no girl?" asked Seekay, as Marian described the happenings of the street. Often, thus, she stood at the small clear-glass spot in the elaborately stained window and interpreted the street scenes to Seekay sitting indolently at his big desk.

"No girl," said Marian. "I think our correspondent, Helen Freel, has changed her mind about coming, all right."

"If she did," Seekay retorted, in the slightly bleak tone that was his when he scented danger, "then her mind was changed—for her!"

Marian continued to gaze into the street, and at the sparse movement there in the late March dusk.

An old man came by, with the heavy walk of age, using his neatly rolled umbrella as a partial crutch. A woman, with white hair showing a little from under a black governess' cap, passed him on the opposite sidewalk. A man in chauffeur's livery, walking toward the lake....

"A cab is slowing up, down the street," Marian said suddenly.

Seekay did not move. His eyes remained closed in the eyeholes of his mask.

"There! The cab has stopped, half a block away. I guess it's not coming here after all. And a man is getting out of it, not a girl."

"Is the man alone in the cab?" asked Seekay, his words a shade faster than before.

"I don't know. I can't see into the cab at this distance. Anyway if there's anyone else there, he, or she, is not getting out."

Seekay's hand moved to a row of buttons on the edge of his desk. He pressed one. Instantly all the noises of the street, greatly amplified, roared through a hidden loudspeaker into the shaded, secluded office. It was as if the room had suddenly been shifted into the center of the roadway.

"...wait here for me...."

That would be the young man at the cab. Steps sounded as he came nearer Seekay's door. From down the block came the two-toned scream of an auto horn, like the cry of a prehistoric monster in a dismal swamp. Then, there came another sound.

Seekay's eyes flew open at it. His hands opened and lay flat on his desk, then his right touched the amplifying button, and the sound came clearer.

"What is it?" whispered Marian, a wrinkle between her level brows. She peered through the spot in the window. The stooped old man with the umbrella had passed beyond her line of vision; she could see nothing but the cab and the young man approaching with rapid, firm steps.

Seekay said nothing, only listened. The sound was a sort of faint creak. Regular, rhythmic, slow. It would have been inaudible save for the amplifier. Creak, creak, creak. There was something ghastly, eerie, about it, though you could not have defined it.

It was a little like the slow, dragging steps of some hideously maimed person, limping on a limb of metal instead of flesh.

"**WHAT IN** heaven's name is it?" Marian repeated in a low tone.

Seekay only shook his head, and listened the more intently to that indefinably hellish sound. Mingled with it were the nearing steps of the man from the cab.

As mysteriously as it had started, the creaking stopped. There was a faint *pouff.*

"Seekay—he's down! The man from the cab—he's down!"

Marian had her face pressed to the window, blue eyes wide.

"My God—he's dead...."

But Seekay wasn't listening. He was out of his chair and leaping for the door of his office, his athletic, tall body fairly hurtling through the air.

He raced through his house vestibule and onto the sidewalk. The blank half-cylinder masking his countenance turned up the street toward where a cab was just pulling away from the curb. He jumped in the same direction.

Two steps took him to a figure lying prone on the cold flagstones of the walk. A young man, with a white, agonized face turned up to the clear, star-studded heaven. Between his eyes was a tiny hole, like a punctuation mark atop the bridge of his nose. He was dead beyond all doubt.

Seekay went on toward the cab with hardly a break in his stride, but it had turned, now, and was racing away up the street. An exclamation came to the lips under the blank pink shield. There was somebody else in the cab. And that somebody else was a girl. He could see her perk, feathered hat—and something else.

A big hand whipping up from the seat beside her and pressing her head back as though brutal fingers had materialized from nowhere to choke from her lips the scream that had risen there.

It was too late to do anything about the cab, and Seekay returned to the dead man on the walk only a few yards from his door. A uniformed patrolman ran up from the far corner.

"What's up, Mr. Seekay? Drunken friend of yours…?"

His voice died as he saw the small hole in the dead man's forehead. He turned the man over. There was no hole in the back of his head. Then both he and Seekay stood up suddenly, and stared at each other.

Faint, bluish fumes were coming from the small hole in the lifeless forehead. It was as though a thunderbolt from hell had struck the man down, and this was the thin, sulphurous haze now emanating.

"What killed him?" The policeman's voice was shaken.

Seekay shook his head, light from streetlamp across the way making moving shadows on the blank pink mask that covered his face.

"I don't know."

"Why was he killed?" persisted the cop.

"I don't know that, either. But I think maybe I'm beginning to guess. It might have something to do with a visit a girl named Helen Freel was about to pay me."

"Who's Helen Freel? Why was she coming—"

"I know nothing definite," Seekay said abruptly. "And I am going to be very busy. Take my word for it that I will help headquarters the moment I can—but right now I have many things that must be done strictly alone."

It spoke volumes for the power of the mysterious operative whom Chicago headquarters resented for his strange ways as much as it respected, that the cop hesitated only a moment before nodding his head.

"Oke, Mr. Seekay. I guess you'll be around when we want you. What'll I do now?"

"Call the homicide squad. Meanwhile, stand here by this man. Don't move him, and don't let anybody touch him." He straightened, and spoke in a low, slow murmur to himself. "Smoke from his head. Faintly bluish vapor seeping from the hole in his skull. And that girl in the cab! Was she Helen Freel? What happened to her?"

Unexpressed in audible words, as he stalked rapidly back toward the house, was the thought: that faint *creaking* sound! What did that have to do with the murder, and what caused the ghostly, rhythmic noise?

CHAPTER TWO

THE INVISIBLE BULLET

SEEKAY AND Marian entered the lobby of a small but select apartment hotel on North State Street. It was the address found in the dead man's pocket. The address, and the fact that the dead man was Robert

McCarthy and had something to do with a retired corporation lawyer named A. J. Freel, had been all that the police could discover from their search of McCarthy's pockets. Seekay had snapped that up, and had come here.

Two homicide men were up in McCarthy's room now. Seekay left the routine investigations to them. He concentrated on the hotel clerk.

"No, sir, Mr. McCarthy didn't live here," the clerk said. "He lived where he worked, out in Barrington at the home of A. J. Freel. He was Freel's private secretary, I think. But it was his habit to come to this hotel and put up occasional week-ends in Chicago, or during his vacations. He's been coming here off and on for about four years."

"This is Wednesday," said Seekay. "So he wasn't here on a week-end trip. And March is a queer time to take a vacation."

The clerk tried politely to hide his curiosity about the mask over the private detective's face. When Seekay left the privacy of his home, which was as rarely as possible, he discarded the blank half-cylinder that covered his features in his office, and wore, instead, a waxen mask that duplicated the human features. But the facelike mask was, at second glance, even more ghastly than the pink blank. It was lean, impassive, gently smiling. And the unchanging regularity of its expression gave it the grim eeriness of a basilisk.

"He wasn't exactly on a vacation this time," the clerk said finally. "It was a kind of layoff. Mr. Freel went on a motor trip, alone, with no particular destination in mind. And he didn't know when he'd get back. An announcement was in the papers the other day. He called Mr. McCarthy up—he was in here last week-end, and told him he could have the time off till he got back from the trip."

Seekay's black eyes glittered under the painted black brows of his mask.

"Fred took a motor trip, no destination, alone, didn't know when he'd get back?"

"Yes, sir, according to the papers, and to McCarthy."

"Have you one of the papers announcing Freel's trip?"

"No. But the announcement was in the *Chicago Free Press*, I know. Maybe in all the papers. Sunday edition."

"Was McCarthy worried by anything, do you know? How did he act? As if he were enjoying his stay?"

The clerk rubbed his jaw.

"That's kind of hard to answer. I didn't know him very well. But it seems to me he was kind of absent-minded for the last few days."

"Anybody come to see him during the last two days—a girl for instance?"

The clerk smiled discreetly.

"There was a girl here this afternoon. But she couldn't have had anything to do with his death," he added hastily. "I know people. And I can tell you this girl was all right. Tall, good-looking, brown eyes. I thought *she* looked worried."

"HOW LONG did she stay up there?"

"She was up in his room about fifteen minutes, I think. That wasn't long ago. Then both of them came down, and they were in a hurry. The girl went into that phone booth there, made a call, and then both of them left—and didn't come back."

"Did McCarthy stay around the hotel much?"

"No, he was out a lot. And I think—though I can't be sure of this—that he went out to Barrington a couple of times."

"To Freel's house?"

"That's the only place in Barrington he'd be going to, I guess. But Freel's house is supposed to be shut up tight, while he's gone. McCarthy told me the servants were given time off, too. So I don't think he got in."

Seekay nodded, the grim tensity of his glittering black eyes contrasting strangely with his pallid, waxen smile.

"Thanks a lot. I think I'll use that booth in the lobby corner myself."

He went inside, and dialed the Chicago Free Press, asking for the city editor.

"Mike, this is Seekay. After information on A. J. Freel. Thumb over the morgue for me, will you?"

There was a pause while the files on Freel were brought to the editor's desk.

"Here you are, Seekay. Quite a lot on Fred. He's a bit of a nut, the kind that makes news.

"Corporation lawyer, retired, worth several million. Widower, childless. Lives alone in Barrington in a cockeyed kind of castle known locally as Freel's Folly. We ran a yarn on it once. He built the thing of concrete, with the declaration that no two straight lines in it should be quite parallel, and that no two rooms should be quite on the same level. The result is that you wander upstairs and down, and never know exactly where you are. Windows stuck in at all sorts of odd places, and heavily barred."

"Afraid of burglars?" asked Seekay.

"Not exactly. According to local gossip, the old man—he's over seventy—is afraid of some kind of upset in the country. Wars and revolutions all around. Thought maybe there'd be a revolution or something here, and he wanted a sort of fort to hide in when it came. For the same reason, he didn't have any use for standard investments, or even for banks. Thought they'd all go smash one day."

"Relatives?"

"One niece, living in New York. I haven't her name—"

"Would it be Helen Freel?"

"It might. I don't know."

"Would A. J. Freel have New York, and a visit to his niece, as a destination on this motor tour of his?"

"Probably," said Mike indifferently.

"But what's up, Seekay?"

"You'll find out any minute," said Seekay. "I'd give it to you over the phone, but it wouldn't be a scoop anyhow, because all the reporters are swarming on it already, including your own. And I'm in a tremendous hurry. Thanks. Goodbye."

He hung up on spluttering exclamations.

"Headquarters," Seekay said absently, getting into his powerful coupe.

Marian took one glance at him and, automatically, got behind the wheel. Often she chauffeured him when he wanted to think as he rode. And he was obviously thinking hard now. His eyes were half-closed under the painted brows of his mask. He spoke aloud to himself.

"Long tour, although he's over seventy. Alone. Servants dismissed for the trip. House tightly closed. Secretary given the time off. Yet his only relative, a niece, is right here in Chicago—and she phoned me with terror in her voice for an appointment."

DETECTIVE GRANN talked to Seekay when he reached headquarters.

"Yeah, we've given this McCarthy bird the once-over, and we don't know a thing. Damnedest business I ever saw. Hole in the front of his head like a bullet hole, only smaller. No hole in the back of his head where the missile came out. Yet there's no bullet, or shot or whatever, in his skull."

"What the devil do you mean?"

"Uh huh. Something went into his head, didn't come out—and yet ain't there."

"When I saw him," Seekay said, "there was a faint bluish vapor rising from the hole in the bone. I suppose your patrolman reported that. Did the coroner find anything that might have made that smoke?"

"Nope. I tell you there wasn't a thing in his skull. If a slug went in there, it just disappeared."

"What does the penetrated portion of the brain look like?"

"The doc said it had a kind of burned look. He said that if a bolt of lightning had killed McCarthy, it might possibly have made such a hole, and have burned the brain stuff like that. But this is March and a clear night. No chance of lightning."

"So precisely nothing has turned up that gives a definite hint as to how McCarthy was killed," said Seekay.

"I'm afraid you got it. What are you going to do now?" said Grann.

"Just think things over," Seekay said evasively.

But as soon as he got down to his coupe, he said to Marian, "Public phone booth at some big store where they'll have a lot of directories."

They entered a teeming downtown drugstore together. Now and then a person turned to look after Seekay, but most, at a casual glance, did not notice that his face was not a face but a mask. The two bent over a counter where directories of neighboring suburbs were stacked. Seekay took up the Barrington book.

"I want to get hold of the butler," he said. "Now, what's the best way?"

Marian smiled a little.

"The butler would order the supplies for Freel's big house," she said. "Unless he's a highly unusual butler, he would get a little rakeoff on groceries and such. That wouldn't be sent to him at the Freel place. It would be sent to his home."

"So the Freel grocer should know the butler's address," nodded Seekay.

He traced down the classified section, picked the name of the grocer with the biggest box advertisement and called it.

"No, I don't get any of Freel's business," the man said who answered the phone. His voice was snappish about it. "I used to. But I don't now. And you can ask Freel's butler why I don't."

"Something to do with a kickback?" suggested Seekay smoothly.

"Everything to do with it! The pirate! He—"

"What I really called you about was to ask the man's address, and full name. Can you tell me?"

"Sure. Freel's butler is a guy named Cronin. James Cronin. He lives at 860 High Street, in Oak Park...."

CHAPTER THREE
THE SECOND DEAD

SEEKAY AND Marian drove out to Oak Park that evening.

James Cronin, butler to A. J. Freel, had a wife, it developed. She opened the door at Seekay's knock. But she opened it fearfully, on a night-chain.

"Who are you? What do you want?"

"I'd like to see your husband if you please."

"He isn't in," she said hastily.

"I believe he is. And I must see him. Police business."

"Police!" She bit her lips till it seemed the blood must come. Then slowly, reluctantly, she unchained the door.

"He's upstairs. I'll tell him you want to see him, but I don't know—he's sick and don't want to talk to anyone." Mrs. Cronin stared fearfully at Seekay's impassive mask. "You wait here."

Seekay heard slow steps upstairs, as someone paced up and down a room. He reached out and stopped the woman as she turned to leave him.

"Don't bother. I'll go up myself."

He turned from her before she had a chance to object and climbed the stairs. He knocked on the door behind which the pacing was sounding. There was an abrupt silence. A tense silence.

Seekay knocked again. "Open the door, please."

"Who's that!" a man's voice yelled. "You can't come in! Get away from the door!"

"Open up," said Seekay quietly, "or I'll be forced to break the door down."

"*You can't come in*—oh, my God—"

Seekay hit the door heavily.

There was the quick snap of a lock and the door was thrown abruptly back.

"All right, then, damn you—*come* in—"

And Seekay found himself facing a maniac.

Freel's butler, a heavy-set man with a face that must normally have been florid but was now flour-white, glared at him with blazing pale eyes. And shaking in his hand was a .45 automatic.

"I'll kill you! I'll kill anybody that…. Oh, why did Maria let you in!"

Seekay stared into the crazed blue eyes.

"I haven't come to hurt you. I've come to help," he said, gently, patiently, as to a child. "I only want to ask you a few questions. It's about this motor trip of your employer, Freel—"

He stopped. To his phenomenally acute ears a sound had suddenly come. A sound which, especially after the bizarre and inexplicable murder of McCarthy, was enough to freeze his blood.

A faint, almost inaudible *creaking*.

Creak, creak, creak. Like the slow walk of a cripple on an artificial leg.

"Well," screamed Cronin, "what the hell are you gawping at—"

Seekay didn't answer. He threw himself suddenly to the floor.

Quick as he was, Cronin's body hit almost as soon. There was a slight *pouff* of sound. That was all. Then Cronin lay motionless between Seekay and the window of the bedroom.

Seekay sprang to his feet. The window was open about four inches. It was from there that the sound had come. And from there must have come whatever it was that struck down the butler. He jumped for the window and threw it up.

He was too late. There was a porch roof under the window, and on this some person had stood. But there was no one on the roof now, and when he clambered out to it and looked at the rear yard, he could still see no one. He went back.

There was a hole in the back of Cronin's head just like that in the forehead of Freel's secretary. From it came faint wisps of bluish vapor....

IN SEEKAY'S big, dim office a strange thing was taking place. At least it seemed inexplicably strange to Marian.

Seekay had a pair of dark blue, almost black, blankets which he was swiftly cutting into strips and squares.

"Why are you doing that?" she couldn't refrain from asking.

"Because the moon is not out tonight," Seekay replied. "It should be quite dark. But I haven't anything black in the house. These blankets are so dark, however, that they will serve the purpose. You'd better take off your clothes."

Marian gasped a little. But she had worked for Seekay for some time now—long enough to obey without question the orders he gave her.

"All my clothes?" was all she said.

"Most of them," Seekay said calmly. "Modesty will be preserved, of course. But pretty scantily. There won't be room under this for much bulk."

Marian had on a brown wool dress. She slipped out of the modishly tightfitting garment, and took off her slip. Besides stockings and shoes, two wisps of peach silk were her only covering. But Seekay didn't even look at her—just went on cutting up the blankets. Yet she was worth looking at, she thought resentfully. You'd think she was a thing of wood, for all Seekay cared....

"You *are* lovely, of course," Seekay said calmly. "But this is scarcely the time for me to say so, is it?"

Pink flamed from Marian's cheeks down her throat. But she had to grin a little at herself. Seekay caught up a big needle and coarse black thread.

"I'm not much of a seamstress, but I think I can fix this costume so you won't burst out of it. Too bad if you did!"

He adjusted a strip of blanket around her shapely right thigh, and rapidly basted a seam up the back. Similarly he encased her left leg, and then the soft curves of her body, touching her smooth whiteness, however, as if she were a figure in marble instead of flesh. She stood, a slimly molded statue in blue-black, like a circus figure in all-covering tights.

"Now you'll do the same for me," said Seekay.

With the pair of them in skin-tight darkness of blanket material, Marian said, "Do you know, I didn't understand till just this minute. We're dressing in black so we can walk in the black, moonless night without running the risk of being seen."

"Excellent," said Seekay, not without irony.

Marian ignored it. "How about sound?" she said. "Oughtn't we to muffle our shoes so we'll be soundless as well?"

"No," said Seekay. "It's not necessary. The cold-blooded devil we're after is partially deaf."

"How on earth do you know that?"

"I know a great deal about this business. And you should too. There are pointers enough.

"**ONE, FREEL,** though an old man, starts off on a motor tour alone with no destination or duration time announced. This fact is given out to the papers, though ordinarily it isn't a thing of enough importance to be printed.

"Two, Freel has his windows barred heavily because he fears some sort of revolution or trouble, and is sure the whole present financial and political set-up will break down soon.

"Three, Freel dismisses servants and secretary for the duration of his trip, instead of simply keeping his house open for his return.

"Four, he leaves in the face of the fact that Helen Freel, his niece and only relative, is—or was—now in his own territory. In other words, as she comes, he goes."

"Well?" Marian said.

"Well, the obvious answer is that Freel has *not* left his house. He didn't go on any trip. He's out in his Barrington place now. Dead. Murdered."

"But—"

"His house was 'shut up' because his murderers wanted the place to themselves. For a similar reason they gave out the news that he was going away on a trip, and they dismissed McCarthy and the servants. So there they are, in a closed and apparently deserted home of steel and concrete which the city editor of the Free Press said was like a fort. They have the run of the place, with little to fear."

Seekay reached up to a high shelf and brought down two things that looked like fish bowls save that they were cylindrical instead of globular, and were made of unbreakable glass. One of them he gave to Marian without comment.

"However," he went on after a moment, "several people seem to have suspected something wrong. McCarthy obviously smelled a rat when he was given leave of absence, probably by someone other than Freel, over the telephone. He pretty certainly tried to get in, out at Barrington, and of course found the place locked tight against him. His actions were such that they caused the murderer, or murderers, to follow him.

"The butler also must have seen or suspected something. He was threatened in such a way as nearly to drive him mad from fright. Later, when it looked as though he might talk to me, the murderer killed him, too, to keep him from saying anything. And as for the girl, Helen Freel….

"We can assume that she went out to Barrington to visit her uncle, found the place closed, and was perplexed enough to seek out McCarthy, her uncle's secretary. He must have told her his suspicions that something was very wrong, after which, from the lobby of McCarthy's hotel, she phoned me and made an appointment. But outside this house McCarthy was killed when he came toward the door first to see that the way was clear, and Helen Freel was kidnapped in her own cab."

"She is… dead… too?" asked Marian in a low voice.

CHAPTER FOUR

THE HOUSE OF DESTRUCTION

SEEKAY SHRUGGED, and turned from Marian for a moment. He slipped off the blank face-shield he wore in his home, and turned back toward her again with his street-mask substituted. The waxen lips smiled gently, with terrible impersonality, as he replied:

"She may be alive—and be praying for death. She may be dead—if the murderers have what they are after."

"*What* are they after? Why did they do all this to get privacy in Freel's home? What's going on in there now?"

"All answered by our listing the pointers now in our possession," said Seekay crisply. "The one about Freel's fearing a crack-up so keenly that he makes a fort of his home. Which, by the way, would make it unlikely that he would *ever* leave that home for any length of time, on a motor trip or anything else. Come on. We're going out to Barrington now."

They got to the Chicago suburb at a few minutes after one in the morning. The night, as Seekay had said, was black.

Seekay wrapped a strip of the dark blanket around Marian's face, so that only her eyes showed. He did the same to his own head. And then he slipped the glass helmets over their heads.

He had stopped the coupe a half-mile from Freel's Folly. They got out and began walking toward it, over great lawns of suburban estates.

They got to the grounds around Freel's home. They could barely pick out the building's outlines against the starry sky. Weird, eccentric outlines. The thing was like a two-story miniature of the walled city of Carcassonne, all slanting turrets and peaked roofs.

Seekay lifted his helmet a little.

"You're to get in first," he whispered. "I want to look over the garage. Then I'll join you. Hunt for the Freel girl."

"How will I get in?" she whispered back. "You say the place is like a fort. If a gang of murderers is in there, it won't be easy to trespass."

"There won't be a gang. At most, two, and I think only one." Seekay's eyes swept over the building's eccentricities. "How athletic are you? Could you climb that rainpipe over there—the one that runs up to that single-barred little gable window—and hang on with one hand while you sawed the bar with the other?"

"Two hours a day in the gymnasium for the last few years says I can," Marian whispered back. "But the window's so small I don't know if I could get through."

"I think you can. But I couldn't. I'll meet you inside later, after I've found another way of entrance."

"Where shall I meet you?" Marian whispered, eyeing the weird building.

"The basement," said Seekay.

He slipped something into her hand—a hacksaw blade. He now held a flashlight as his only weapon. No gun. There were no pockets in their odd black get-ups. She had a tiny flash, too.

"But don't use it unless it's essential," Seekay whispered, guessing uncannily at her thoughts as he often did. "Our man is deaf, but there's nothing wrong with his eyesight! By the way, *look out for the umbrella!*"

Then he was gone, a black figure melting into the blackness of the night.

SEEKAY SLIPPED to the low, flat-roofed addition to the rear of Freel's Folly whose wide doors told that it was the garage. The windows of this addition were as impregnable, as heavily barred, as those of the house proper; so Seekay didn't bother with them. He went to the small door set beside one of the big garage doors, and bent low down.

He scratched lightly at the portal, and whined a little. There was no sound in the garage. He repeated the process, scratching more loudly. When there was still no response of any kind, he drew from a crude sleeve the needle with which he had sewed the blanket strips, and bent to the lock. He had the garage door unlocked in less than ten minutes.

In all that time, he had heard no sound in the garage, but he was still not satisfied that no one was in there. By his reasoning, there should be. It was highly improbable that the man who had killed McCarthy and Cronin would lurk in the great house without a guard of some sort. And what better place for a guard than in the garage, which was the most vulnerable point of entrance, and where a car, means of a getaway in case something went wrong, stood ready?

He took off the glass helmet, opened the door, and poked the helmet slowly into the garage's blackness.

There was a smashing impact on it that jarred his arm clear up to his shoulder. Then snarled words. "Yeah! Thought you were so smart. I guess *that* cooks you—"

Seekay's fist smashed against a dim white blotch which was the speaker's face. The blotch sagged down as the man fell to his knees. Seekay struck again; and heard a sickening snap. Without a second look, he stepped over the body.

MARIAN STOOD in blackness that was like fetid water. The room behind the little gable window was so dark that the blackness seemed stifling.

She rubbed her right arm. It was numb with the work of sawing that bar over the window. Quite a job, hanging onto a pipe with your left hand and sawing an inch bar with your right! She'd almost given it up before the bar came loose in her hand. She held it now, like a club.

She listened intently, and could hear nothing. She was, she admitted to herself, scared white. Something terrible, something as horrible as it was mysterious, must be going on in the black depths of this strange house. What? She had no notion. But that there was a killer here—a person who seemed able to deal death from afar with the eerie certainty of a bolt from hell—was pretty positive.

In the tomblike quiet and darkness, Marian started to tiptoe away from the window, hand outstretched. Her foot touched something that rattled noisily. She moved to the left and touched something else that scraped along the floor. Yet when she felt ahead of her with her hand, she found that she could touch nothing.

She pressed the switch of her little flashlight for a half-second. The beam revealed a strange thing.

The floor was littered with what had been the furnishings of the room. But those furnishings were in pieces, now. In fantastically small bits.

There had been several chairs and a bed in the little room. They were sawed again and again. Chair-legs in a dozen pieces. Bed-posts the same way. Chair upholstery ripped as if a demented monster, filled with the urge to destroy, had been confined in the room.

The bizarre ferocity that had made kindling of the furniture, had extended to the walls and floor. Every third floorboard was ripped up. The walls were slashed in ir-regular lines every six inches or so. The sidelamps of the room had been torn out by the sockets.

In the brief instant that her flash had been on, Marian had seen that the door of the room was open. She crept toward it.

As she almost fell down three short steps, she played the flash again for a second. The second ray of light showed that she had not stepped down from the little gable room into a hail, as one would expect, but into a second, larger room. The flash had showed more sawed furniture, more gashed walls, more ripped flooring.

And something else. Something that drove the breath suddenly back down Marian's throat till it seemed she must suffocate.

A man's foot, sticking toe-up from behind a mound of rubble over which the drapes torn from the windows had been thrown. The foot had been very still—terribly still.

MARIAN BIT her lip to gather the courage that Seekay seemed to think she possessed, and she forced herself to tip-toe toward that foot. She got to the mound of rubble in the dark. She felt around it, and choked down a cry as her hand touched a face in the blackness. A cold, dead face.

She gathered up some of the ripped drapes on the mound, and made a little funnel with her flash in the middle. With this hiding her light, she hoped, she trained a small beam on the face.

It was that of an old man. Freel himself, almost certainly. And he must have been dead for days. But there was no small hole in his head, as there had been in the heads of the others. There was no mark at all on his face.

She moved the flash further along the old man's body. No sign of blood. No sign of violence....

She nearly dropped the flash. She had got down to the withered right hand of the body, now. And she saw that the fingers of this hand had no nails. There was pulpy flesh where the nails should be, and ugly little trickles of dried blood. The nails had been pulled out.

She turned out the flash and started to get up. She must go to the basement to meet Seekay. Then she froze, motionless. Suddenly it seemed her heart must stop its wild beating.

A low, thin moan came to her ears through the shuddering blackness. It was like the ghost of a cry for help. Just the one eerie, thin sound, then silence....

Silence for about ten seconds, after which there was another slight sound. And at this one the length of iron bar slid from Marian's lax fingers and her horror increased ten-fold. For this, following hard on the slight, agonized moan, was a faint, almost inaudible *creaking* noise.

Creak, creak, creak.

The same sound, somehow rasping each nerve-end with a message of death, that she had heard just before Freel's secretary was murdered. The same sound Seekay had heard just before Cronin went down with a tiny hole in his head from which came wisps of vapor, like the fumes of hell itself.

Creak, creak....

Marian's quivering hand pointed her flash toward the sound, and pressed the little switch. Death to reveal her position in the room like this? Doom, if she made of herself a target? She didn't care—or even stop to think of that. All she knew was that she couldn't stand the blackness, the unplaced creaking which twice before had spelled bizarre murder, any longer.

A pencil flame of white rayed from the small flash. And intuition, or a sense of hearing keener than she normally knew, must have guided her hand, for the beam rested squarely on a figure in the other doorway of the room....

The figure of a man, crouched as if ready to spring, powerful, youthful, with a mop of brown hair disarranged over a face—a face that was contorted into the incarnation of sadistic fury! A laugh of pure hysteria leaped to Marian's lips as she saw that this figure, his cold pig-like eyes glaring murder at her, had in his hands—an umbrella.

Not a gun, or dagger. Not a deadly weapon. But a tight-rolled, average-looking black umbrella!

CHAPTER FIVE

THE UMBRELLA'S SECRET

WITH HIS lips snarling curses, the man flung the umbrella up, pointing it straight at her head, dimly to be seen in the backwash of her flash. Only then did Seekay's words recur to her: *Look out for the umbrella!*

She started to drop to the floor to get away from that menacing tip, but was too late. Something banged against her helmet with a force that snapped her head back on her shoulders. Simultaneously she heard a thin, brittle tinkling as if a chandelier had broken in a thousand pieces.

Then she was on her knees, dazed by the shock against her helmet, staring helplessly up at the maniac that was rushing toward her with the umbrella furiously clubbed. She read death in his figure....

But then there was movement behind the man, and a white hole in the blackness as a flash was turned on in the doorway where the man had first stood. In the new light, Marian could see Seekay's mask, gently smiling, imperturbable, while his flashlight played on the killer, who had whirled from her with the first stabbing ray.

The man pointed his umbrella, gunlike, at Seekay. And Seekay, with his smiling mask a monstrous thing in the face of the peril of the umbrella's threat, deliberately and slowly walked forward.

"Stop! Get back, or I'll kill you!"

The killer's voice was hysterical.

Seekay's black eyes glittered a little more brightly through the eyeholes of his mask.

"Stop—damn you—"

Seekay kept on coming, step by step, till finally the killer broke. He screamed like a madman and sprang at Seekay with the queer weapon clubbed.

The umbrella crashed down. Seekay staggered a little, but kept on, protected by his helmet. And now he was in reach. Horribly, with a sort of fiendish irrelevancy, his painted waxen mouth continued to smile—while his powerful hands took the murderer's throat in a deadly clasp. It kept on smiling as the killer gurgled and writhed in that viselike clutch. At length Seekay's hands reluctantly opened and he dropped the slack body.

"Can't kill him," she heard his voice, muffled by his fantastic helmet. "Better the chair for him."

There was a period in which things swam around Marian and she saw only hazily. Saw Seekay stride to a nearby lamp, which lay on the floor with its base ripped in two. Saw him wrench the cord loose and bind the man with it. Saw him experimentally snap the light-switch in the wall near the door, and saw the room flooded with brilliance from an overhead light which, though ripped loose from its ceiling fixture, still functioned.

"Not so smart," Seekay said, staring at the unconscious figure on the floor. "The place was supposed to be closed indefinitely, yet you forgot to have the electricity turned off."

SEEKAY CAME to Marian, then, and helped her up. In the strong circle of his arm she began to feel normal again. She took off her helmet when she saw him take off his.

Seekay strode to the umbrella and picked it up. He nodded.

"An air gun. And a very powerful one. I thought it must be the umbrella. And a single-shot...."

Marian's lips parted. Seekay forestalled her question.

"At dusk a man was killed outside our house. Killed silently by a missile of no known caliber. That suggested an air gun. Carried by whom? The position of the body showed that the shot could not have come from the cab, but had probably been fired by someone on the sidewalk. A moment before, among other passersby, you mentioned an old man with an umbrella. An umbrella, though the sky was cloudless and there was no sign of rain. It was almost a certainty that he was the killer and the umbrella was an air gun."

He held the fabric roll of the umbrella in his left hand, and moved down on the crook-handle with his right. A faint, almost inaudible creak resulted as the handle slipped down on the metal shaft. Marian cried out a little at the associations of the sound. But Seekay only said:

"Of course. The creaking sounded when he pumped up the gun for a shot. Which meant that he was deaf. For that gun was pumped in circumstances where silence would be imperative, and the fact that he didn't hear the creak and stop it with a drop of oil could only mean that he wasn't able to hear it. And here's the trigger... the little catch you press when you want to open it. An ordinary catch when the gun wasn't loaded—a trigger after it had been pumped up."

Seekay paused and bent over the bound man, feeling in his pockets. He brought out a small black case, like a cigarette case only thrice as thick. It had a cork lining, a second lid, and under that, a little gray globule like a dull moonstone. There were depressions for two more of the globules.

"Dry ice" said Seekay. "Lead pellets might have been traced to his umbrella gun. Ice would penetrate bone, given enough force, and then would melt and leave no damning clue. Dry ice, forming vapor as it melts, was best because it lasted longest in his insulated case. I thought it was ice. Hence our glass helmets, which would have been no protection against regular bullets, of course...."

Marian heard again a sound she had forgotten for the moment. A low, thin moan from the next room.

Seekay jumped to the door.

A girl lay on the ripped-up floor near a ventilator grate. Her wide brown eyes were sick with pain and terror. On her lips was adhesive tape, which not quite silenced her. Her left foot was a mass of blisters where she had been tortured.

"Helen Freel!" said Seekay, bending over her with gentle sympathy. "I heard her moan, down that ventilator shaft, while I was waiting for you in the basement. That's why I came up—"

He ripped off the tape, and unbound her. She fainted. He picked her up and carried her downstairs, with Marian following.

Everywhere was the same ferocious destruction she had seen before. Furnishings sawed and smashed to bits.

"Why did that... that murderer hate Freel so?" she said.

SEEKAY STARED at her over his pathetic burden. "Haven't you got it yet? Freel lived in this fort because he thought everything was going to hell in this country. He distrusted the whole set-up—including banks. Would he, then, keep his fortune in banks? No. He'd keep it under his own roof, in some tangible form that he could lay his hands on. Not cash. That could become worthless too. Precious metals, gems, I don't know what. But that man with the umbrella knew of Freel's hoard and came here to get it. He started to torture Freel, when he had cleared the house for action, and Freel died. So he ripped the place to pieces in his effort to find Freel's treasure. When he kidnapped Helen Freel in front of our office, he didn't kill her at once. He brought her here on the faint chance that she knew the hiding place and might be forced to tell."

They were in the front of the place, now, in a big hall from which the front door led out to the terrace.

Seekay set Helen Freel down and went to the phone.

He passed the phone and stood before it. The door was open—the killer had of course searched in there during his attempt to unearth whatever treasure Freel had. But the door had not been forced in any way. It was unmarred. And that was odd.

Seekay picked up the bent metal cover of a base-plug that had been ripped out of the wall, and scraped at the black enamel on the iron box. Then, for several seconds, he stared wide-eyed at the exposed metal composing the safe.

"Platinum," he said. "Solid platinum! Probably the whole safe—a thousand pounds or more of the precious metal! Set right out here in the front hall. Who'd dream the safe itself was the thing of value instead of what it might contain? And Freel, to guarantee against a burglar's jimmying it and exposing the metal, left the combination open so that thieves' hands could swing the door at will and see that nothing of value was inside."

He picked up the phone, ascertained that it was working, and called headquarters. Helen Freel moaned and opened her eyes. "Tom Franca… uncle's chauffeur… killing me… where…."

"He can't hurt any one now," said Seekay. "So the driver was the one who decided to root out the fortune Freel refused to trust to banks, eh?"

"Yes. Dismissed by my uncle for deafness. Angry…."

"The devil," Seekay said, as her eyes closed once more.

"She'll be all right," said Marian, a shade resentfully. "Worry about *me* a little, will you?"

Seekay's arm went around her slender, black-clad body hard, for an instant. His eyes were less grim than usual in the eyeholes of his perpetually smiling mask.

"I guess you know without being told what I went through when I saw that inventive devil charging toward you."

Marian thrilled to the brief, hard arm pressure. Such a thing was rare with Seekay. And marvelously nice. She wondered what it would be like to have a husband without any face.

TWO TICKETS TO HELL

A THIN, CRIMSON FROTH
FLECKING THEIR LIPS, THOSE
TWO AIRLINE PASSENGERS WERE
FOUND, MURDERED BY A DRUG
THAT LEFT NO SLIGHTEST TRACE.
ONLY SEEKAY COULD SOLVE
WHAT SEEMED A MOTIVELESS
DEATH-RIDDLE. SO HE MADE TWO
RESERVATIONS FOR A FLIGHT TO
HELL, AND HE WORE A CORPSE'S
FACE!

CHAPTER ONE
THE WITNESS
IS A CORPSE

THOUGH IT was broad afternoon outside, the room was almost totally dark. Eerie darkness, it was, in which book-lined walls and huge desk—and the figure seated behind the desk—were only dimly seen.

In the gloom, a deep-toned, mellow bell sounded, like a chapel bell in a graveyard at midnight. Then another bell, lighter in tone, joined its peal.

Seekay stirred in his chair. Seekay—the world's most unique private detective. Faint streaks of light from the nearest shaded window rested on him, then. And his secretary and right-hand "man" Marian Ford, caught her breath as she always did at the sight of her weird employer.

Seekay had no face.

For the rest, he was a normal figure of a man; tall, broad-shouldered, immaculately clad. His hair, thick black and shot through with a little grey, grew crisply back from his high intelligent forehead. His hands were powerful, square, long-fingered. His body moved as that of a young, athletic man. But his face.... Where his face should have been there was only a blank celluloid shield, covering his countenance from below the chin to the hairline.

No one knew what lay under that curved pink shield. Deformed monstrosity? Noseless, mouthless ruin? What? No one could guess. But the oddity of a shield where a face should have been was the reason why Seekay's office was usually in semi-darkness.

The deep-toned bell pealed again. The lighter, more highly-pitched bell had never ceased ringing.

"Some one at our door," said Marian Ford, rather unnecessarily. She was a very lovely person, with tawny brown hair and dark blue eyes and a body that made most men turn to look after her as she walked lithely down a sidewalk. But not Seekay. His black, arrogant eyes, staring through the eyeholes of his bizarre shield, never seemed to notice her.

"Yes," said Seekay. "Some one at our door. Press the buzzer so that he can come in."

Seekay lunged forward, facing death....

Marian's eyebrows went up over puzzled blue eyes. This was not like Seekay, to see a person merely because that person rang his doorbell. Usually the private detective, who was wealthy independently of his practice, saw callers only under the most unusual circumstances. Now, he was opening his door at the first summons!

"You are sure you don't want me to ask who it is and what he wants to see you about?" she said.

Seekay's head shook, sending little dim glints of light from the enigmatic pink face-shield.

"I know what he wants to see me about," he said. "He wants to kill me. Let him in at once."

Marian gasped. "Wants to—kill you?"

"Yes, of course!" Seekay's voice was impatient. "You hear that lighter ringing, over the peal of the doorbell itself? You should know what that means."

Marian bit her red lip. She did know, but had forgotten for the moment. It was the warning peal of a photo-electric cell device newly installed in Seekay's vestibule which detected the presence of any sizeable bit of metal. Such as a knife or gun.

"The door, please!" Seekay snapped, with more than impatience in his tone now. "Would you keep a murderer waiting?"

MARIAN WENT quickly out of the office and down the hall toward the vestibule, after pressing the release spring opening the inner door to the visitor. She went quickly—but dreaded going. A man to kill Seekay. And he calmly let him in. Increasingly Marian, whose blue eyes had of late taken on a tender light when they rested on Seekay's facelessness, worried about the cold recklessness of her boss.

Toward her, down the hall, came a man whose hat was off politely and whose face was twisted in a smile. But a man from whom instinctively she would have run had she met him in a dark and lonely place. His body was under-sized and flashily clad. His face was as sharp as a chisel, and about as kindly. His eyes, trying to be amiable, were cold and still. They were not normal.

"In here, please," Marian found herself saying.

She led the way into Seekay's office. The caller blinked in the dim light. He stared across the huge desk at the weird figure with only a pink shield for a face. Marian stood to one side.

"You're Seekay?" the caller said, walking slowly toward the desk.

"Yes," came the eerie detective's deep, calm voice.

The man was within a yard of the desk. He stopped, and stood motionless. "Yeah, you'd be him, all right," he said. "I was told what you looked like. I got something special for you—*and here it is!*"

With the last words, far too quickly for any possible precaution to have been taken by Seekay, his hand whipped from under the hat he carried. In the hand was a silenced revolver. On his face was a snarling grin of death.

Marian screamed softly, but the gun didn't spit lead. Instead, it suddenly dipped down and forward, clear out of line with Seekay, and the gangster yelled like an echo to Marian's scream. Then he dropped the gun as if it had burned him, and the gun shot through the air to the end of the desk, and hung there as if suspended on a nail. Only no nail was in evidence.

Seekay got up leisurely and started toward the killer. The killer yelled again, this time more hoarsely. Seekay was walking deliberately, right through the desk. Then he utterly disappeared, as if he had stepped through a window into space. The murderer was too paralyzed to cry out again as, without warning, his hands were wrenched behind him and handcuffed.

He turned and stared at Seekay.

"My God," he croaked, "how'd you get around behind me?"

"I've been behind you from the start," shrugged the faceless detective. "You only saw me in a mirror placed behind my desk. Your gun was snatched from you by a powerful magnet, which now holds it securely clamped against the side of the desk—which is metal, not wood. Curious how the simplest tricks are most effective." His voice took on a steely edge. "Who are you? Why did you try to kill me?"

The chisel-like features of the weedy gunman hardened. This was stuff he could understand—and defy.

"Don't you wish you knew!" he mocked.

"You'd better tell me."

"Nice June weather we're having, ain't it?" sneered the man.

His sneer faded under the detective's deadly stare.

"I think we'll find out," said Seekay softly. "My methods of questioning are not police methods...."

The telephone bell rang softly on Seekay's desk. Marian stared inquiringly at him. He nodded.

"It will be a case," he said, "and we shall accept it."

AGAIN MARIAN felt bewilderment grip her. Seekay only rarely took cases, and then simply because their odd or mad features appealed to his sense of the bizarre. Now, he was accepting a job in advance—if this phone call indeed were the offer of one.

She went to the desk, but did not lift the phone. She put on a head-set instead, and picked up pencil and short-hand pad. Seekay it was who took the telephone. The gunman, attention off him, instantly darted for the door, handcuffs and all, and found that the panel had been locked somehow, though he'd seen no hand touch it since entering. He stood dejectedly and watched the faceless detective.

"Seekay speaking," Seekay said.

Marian heard an agitated man's voice crackle over the line: "This is Robert Vinton talking. I would like urgently to see you. Will you come to my place at once?"

Marian stared covertly at her employer. Seekay hated to leave his house in daylight. People stared so curiously at his facelessness. This time he agreed without an instant's hesitation.

"I shall come at once. Your address, please?"

Robert Vinton gave it, a number on Chicago's fashionable Michigan Avenue, and Seekay hung up. His eyes were sardonic on Marian's, but he explained patiently.

"You're wondering why I'm so agreeable, of course. It's because of this gentleman's visit." He nodded toward the alert killer. "Obviously he was sent to murder me before I could take this case, which some one knew in advance was to be offered me. If the case is that interesting, I'll work on it, sight unseen."

"And our friend?" murmured Marian.

"We'll extend hospitality to him till we come back."

Seekay stepped to a door in the office wall. He opened it and revealed a shallow closet.

"Hey!" said the killer, suddenly more afraid than he had ever been before in his cheap gangster's life. "You can't hold me here! That's kidnap or somethin'! You got to turn me over to the cops, or...."

Seekay thrust him, still protesting, into the closet.

"Didn't I tell you my methods weren't police methods?" Seekay said gently. "You'll stay here till we return—and then you'll talk. I guarantee it. Meanwhile, yell if you like."

He closed the door on a shout, and turned to Marian.

She got hat and gloves and purse. Seekay joined her at the vestibule door, prepared for the street. His preparations were simple. He had put on another mask. He didn't wear the blank celluloid shield outside; that would have been too conspicuous. In its place was a clever synthetic mask of a face showing gently smiling lips, classic nose and eyebrows, and a regular, firm jaw. But only a second glance was necessary to reveal that this "face" was artificial. You can't fake such things.

Seekay drove in his huge coupe to the given address. An alarmed looking young man with horn-rimmed glasses let him and Marian into a luxuriously appointed, large, top-floor apartment. The man's eyes widened behind his glasses as he stared at the imitation face, but he only said, "You're Detective Seekay?… Good. Mr. Vinton will be *very* glad to see you."

MARIAN AND Seekay followed him into a library. Two men were in there. One was elderly, with a pallor indicating poor health. The other, about forty, tanned, shrewd of face and eye, Seekay recognized. Doctor Frick, fashionable but excellent physician. There was a half-emptied scotch-and-soda on the desk in front of Frick. He had a stethoscope in his hand.

"Seekay," said the elderly man. "I'm Vinton. This—" he nodded toward the young fellow with glasses—"is Mr. Hines, my secretary; and this is Doctor Frick."

"We're acquainted," nodded Seekay. "How are you, Doctor? You know my assistant, Miss Ford?"

Hines had a chair behind Seekay. The detective sat down and looked at him. Hines' eyes were as agitated as Vinton's. Evidently the younger man was deeply attached to him. The doctor finished his highball and stared at Seekay too.

"Thank God you've come," said Vinton to Seekay. "I must have the services of a man like you."

"What service do you require?" asked Seekay.

"Tonight, at eleven, I am to leave my apartment for the airport to catch the eleven-forty-five plane for Florida," said Vinton. "I want you to come with me—guard me on the trip."

Marian glanced quickly at Seekay, expecting him to rise and leave after an indifferent, perhaps annoyed, refusal. The great Seekay, asked to be a simple bodyguard on a trip south! But once more Seekay surprised her.

"All right, I will," he said. "But why do you think you need a guard—"

The outer door opened and a girl came into the room, stopping short in surprise at the strange looking man seated beside the table. She was pretty, almost as beautiful as Marian Ford; a light blonde with large hazel eyes.

"This is my ward, Katherine Hart," said Vinton. "No, stay, Kathy. You needn't leave. You're in this, I feel."

Vinton turned to Seekay again.

"Why do I think I need a guard? I can't tell you definitely. I've only a hunch.... You remember what happened to a man named Hobart, on the north side a few weeks ago?"

Seekay nodded, eyes suddenly hard as jet. There was probably no one in Chicago who didn't know the Hobart case. A moderately wealthy bachelor living near the lake, he had been found by a friend, dead, not quite three weeks ago. But so peculiarly dead! There were marks on his body only in one spot—his throat. But these marks seemed more uncanny than deadly.

Hobart's throat had been described by the newspapers as looking as if it had been lightly brushed with gold leaf. The skin was a strange, greenish-gold color. No explanation had been given.

"I know what happened to Hobart," Seekay said. "He was apparently strangled to death in some inexplicable manner. At least that was the coroner's report—"

He stopped. Katherine Hart had gone pale as chalk.

"I'm sorry," Vinton cut in quickly. "I shouldn't have brought that up. Perhaps you'd better leave after all, Kathy."

She shook her head, lips carefully composed. Vinton sighed.

"Hobart was her uncle," he said gently to Seekay. "But the point I meant to bring up was this: Hobart was on the eve of the same trip I'm planning, when he was killed. A plane trip to Florida. And he was going there for the same reason."

"And that reason?" said Seekay.

Vinton hesitated, glancing at the girl and then away. "I'll… I'll tell you if you insist, but I'd rather not."

"You needn't," said Seekay. He looked at his watch. "It is half-past four now. Shall I stay with you till you leave here for the airport?"

Vinton shook his head. "Not necessary. I'm safe in here. I won't let a soul in till you come back—say, at ten?"

"Make it eight," said Seekay. "You fear you'll be killed the same way Hobart was, for the same reason—to keep you from getting into that Florida plane. I think your fear has a deadly foundation for being. See you at eight…. By the way, Doctor, Mr. Vinton is in good enough health to stand the altitude of an air trip?"

Frick nodded. "Quite good enough. I have just made sure."

SEEKAY LEFT, with young Hines closing the door after him and Marian. Hines' eyes were almost haunted with fear for Vinton. They heard him double-lock the door when it had shut.

"You'll be returning at eight, you say?" Marian asked, as they got into Seekay's enormous coupe.

"I said eight, but I'll be back sooner. The moment I've finished questioning the man we left in the closet, in fact. I wouldn't have left Vinton at all if it hadn't been for our prisoner."

Seekay's voice was grim. Marian wondered what his real expression was behind the painted lips that always, perforce, gently smiled.

"Vinton is in deadly danger," said Seekay. "So, I think, is the girl."

"Katherine Hart?"

"Yes. Hobart, it seems, was killed to keep him from making the Florida trip. Vinton fears he'll be killed to keep him from going. The reason for the trip concerns the girl, of course."

"How do you know that?"

"Didn't you see the way Vinton glanced at her when he said he'd rather not tell the reason for the trip? The reason concerns her. Hobart, her uncle, dead—Vinton, her guardian, fearing death—Well, we'll get some information out of the chap who tried to kill me."

But there was to be no information from that source.

Seekay strode to the office and to the closet door with his hat still on his head, so anxious was he to question the man and hurry back to Vinton. Marian followed at a little distance. Seekay opened the closet door, and Marian's panted exclamation sounded in the dimly lit room.

The man was there, all right. But he didn't walk out when the door was opened. He fell out, straight forward on his face, with his nose plowing into the thick carpet.

Seekay turned him over. There was a bloody froth around the man's mouth and nostrils. He was dead.

CHAPTER TWO
THE DEADLY
IMPERSONATION

SEEKAY, IN white, at his laboratory bench with Marian beside him, straightened from a little test-tube. There was blood in the tube, drawn from the dead man's veins. The blood had been normal red when Seekay began his testing. It was still, obstinately, a normal red, in spite of all the chemicals the faceless detective had added to test for poisons.

"As far as autopsy will show," he said, "this man died naturally. Not a trace of poison in him. Yet he was certainly poisoned, most subtly, before ever he came to my house. The man who hired him to kill me planted death in him so that, successful or not, he would never be able to talk."

"But if he were poisoned, wouldn't there *have* to be traces?" asked Marian.

Seekay shook his head, black eyes clouded.

"There are some poisons, known to very few, that do not leave chemical traces. I think the one used in this instance was *oenanthe crocata*, or hemlock water-dropwort. The bloody foam around the dead mouth, and the white appearance of the pharynx and gullet would indicate that."

On the bench next to the tube with the blood in it, was a pint whiskey bottle half empty. It was an expensive brand

and Seekay had taken it from the man's pocket. Evidently the gunman had sought Dutch courage from the bottle before coming in to kill. Seekay poured the half-pint from the bottle into a curved silver flask and slipped it into his hip pocket.

"There may be traces of something in this liquor," he said. "I'll give it to the police laboratory for testing when we get the time. Take care of that liquor bottle. It may be important, too...."

The extension phone in the laboratory buzzed softly. Seekay took it up. "Yes?"

Marian could hear the voice on the other end, very shaky, almost indistinguishable.

"Seekay? Vinton talking. Don't wait till tonight to get here. Come at once—and for God's sake, come fast!"

There was a click, and Seekay was holding a dead phone. He dropped it in its cradle and fairly ran to one corner of the laboratory.

"What's wrong? Oh, what's the matter?" breathed Marian.

"Plenty! Get that small black bag. It will be big enough."

Marian brought the bag in question, a thing like an overnight bag, but empty of trimmings. Seekay put into it a lump of stuff that looked like rubbery wet clay, and ran from the laboratory, shedding his white coat as he moved.

Marian usually drove when they went out, but Seekay took the wheel himself when he wanted to speed. He took it now, and the huge coupe began sliding along at seventy.

"Will we be in time? What's happened?" Marian gasped.

Seekay's jet-black eyes were intent on the street.

"Vinton is dead," he said. "That is what has happened. Hence, we will not be in time."

"How do you know that? The girl—what about her—"

Seekay screeched to a stop before Vinton's building. At the top floor apartment he rang the bell only once—Then he whipped out a curved blue blade like a thick needle. He entered in less than ten seconds, ruining the lock. He ran to the library.

At the door, his haste ceased. Obviously there was no need for it. Feet and legs of some one lying on the floor could be seen protruding from behind Vinton's library table. The posture shrieked of death. Seekay started forward.

From behind the table, where she had been crouching out of sight, Katherine Hart rose.

Her face was blanched and bloodless, and looked like that of a sleepwalker. Her hazel eyes rested on Seekay's gently smiling mask without really seeing it. She was stunned, out of her mind with horror.

"I killed him," she whispered. "Me! I killed him...."

Seekay went around the desk. It was Vinton who lay dead, all right.

"Keep back," Seekay said to Marian. "It's not pretty."

HOBART HAD been found, as the papers phrased it, with his throat looking as if lightly sprayed with gold dust. Now, Vinton's dead throat had the same curious aspect. It appeared to have been lightly dusted with green-gold leaf. But in a moment Seekay saw the reason, which had not been dwelt on in Hobart's murder.

Vinton's throat looked like that because in its entirety, from chin to collar-bone, it was bruised. The greenish yellow color of the flesh resulted from the even, light bruising which, in death, took on that eerie hue. But what in the name of heaven could have made the gigantic bruise? It looked as if a single enormous hand had constricted on the man's throat. But no hand could have been that big.

Vinton's left cuff was unbuttoned, although for the rest he was immaculately dressed and ready, even that early, to go to the airport. Seekay noticed that as he took the rubbery stuff from his black bag. He pressed the substance carefully down on Vinton's dead face, drew it carefully off again and put it in a compartment of the bag so that it would not move or mash.

"I killed him; I'm a murderer! I killed him...."

Katherine Hart was babbling the words like a broken phonograph. Seekay stared at her, and now it was the turn of *his* eyes to look without really seeing. In their jet black depths cold knowledge was growing.

The knowledge changed suddenly to alertness and tensity as sounds came from the hall outside the apartment.

A voice. That of young Hines. "I'm sure something is wrong. I just stepped out, when the doctor left, a half hour ago, to run an errand for Mr. Vinton before he took his plane trip. When I got back and rang, he didn't open the door. Yet I know he'd have let me in."

A deeper voice said something indistinguishable. Hines' voice sounded a second time, wild with anxiety.

"He'd have let *me* in all right. The fact that he didn't must mean that he can't. And that means.... He was terribly afraid of something. Look! The lock!"

Seekay was next to the outer door, now. He flattened against the wall as the door was burst open. Two uniformed patrolmen leaped in, guns drawn, warned by the broken lock.

Seekay moved like fluid light. Both hands went out. Each caught one of the men on the back of the neck, in a jiu-jitsu blow that knocked both out like stunned rabbits, before either had seen who attacked him. In the hail, Hines stood with bulging eyes. All he'd seen, at that angle, was a pair of hands flashing out, and the two policemen falling. He screamed suddenly, and turned and raced down the hall.

Marian had Katherine by the arm.

"Out to the car with her, quick!" said Seekay.

THEY RACED down the stairs, with Hines' cries ahead of them. They got out the building door, with Katherine between them, as Hines staggered blind with terror along the walk, calling for help. They were away from there in the big coupe before the first of the crowds drawn by the horrified secretary's cries.

"I killed him," whispered Katherine, lips trembling as she sat between the two in the coupe. "Oh, I murdered him!"

"Why," said Marian, "did you knock out the men and run? All the police know Seekay. You wouldn't have been accused of Vinton's murder."

"But Katherine Hart would," said Seekay, speeding toward home. "Listen to her!"

"I killed him. I loved him, but I killed him. Like Uncle Dan Hobart…."

"For the moment she's insane," said Seekay. "A hard-boiled police grilling might easily change that temporary insanity to permanent madness. Prolonged shock does that, sometimes. I couldn't have that happen to an innocent girl."

"How do you know she's innocent?"

"Because I know who is guilty," said Seekay. "But the police don't—yet. So they'd take Miss Hart's delirious words as nine-tenths of a confession and try to force the rest out of her. Hence, I went to a bit of risk to get her out of there unarrested."

"Why in the world is she saying she killed him if she didn't?"

Seekay's fixed lips smiled gently, as they had smiled on the horror of Vinton's discolored throat, as they smiled on everything, unable to change their painted expression.

"It is evident that she thinks she is morally responsible for his death even if not literally responsible," he said. "Similarly, she feels guilty of the death of her uncle, Hobart. Why? Well, let us say that she asked Hobart to do something that resulted in his death. Then she asked Vinton to do the same thing. With both killed, her sense of guilt is overwhelming."

"The trip to Florida! That's what she asked of them!"

"Obviously. The average person does not go to Florida in June without some reason other than amusement."

"What will you do with her?" asked Marian.

"Keep her at the house till her mind clears beyond the chance of being thrown permanently off-balance by machine-gun questions," said Seekay. "You shall take care of her till eleven o'clock. By then she'll probably be safely asleep during the time we are out."

"We're going out at eleven?"

"We're going out at eleven," nodded Seekay. And after that he volunteered no more.

AT HIS house on the near north side, Seekay gave Katherine Hart a sedative and put her to bed. Then he went to the big, cluttered room that was his laboratory. He took from the black bag the rubbery-clay substance which he had pressed over the dead face of Vinton. Into this he washed a thin, opaque stuff like collodion, which coated the cast of the clay in a thin sheet. Taking this out, he had a perfect death cast of Vinton; a face needing only tinting to make it fairly lifelike.

"You knew before you left here to go to Vinton's that he was dead," Marian accused. "So you went prepared to take that cast—for some reason. How did you know?"

Seekay shrugged. "Quite simple. The person phoning us as Vinton, and urging me to hurry to the house—was not Vinton. I recognized a different voice. My hearing is sensitive."

"But why on earth—"

"It was a trap, for Katherine," said Seekay rather impatiently. "I was to hurry there, find her with her dead guardian, and arrest her for his murder. Also for the murder of Hobart, since both were killed in the same seemingly mysterious way. The real murderer couldn't know that in her delirium she would seem to *confess* murder—that was too much of a break. But it wouldn't have been necessary. Her presence there would have been enough for her to be held by the police."

Carefully Seekay tinted the thin mask. When it had been done to his satisfaction, he hung it up to dry.

"It wouldn't fool any one except from a distance, but then that's all it will be asked to do," he remarked rather cryptically.

He picked up the telephone and called headquarters. Marian looked her surprise. In harboring Katherine Hart, he was concealing a murderess, as far as any proof existed to the contrary. Yet he called the police.

He got Detective Grann, a bluff, hard-voiced sergeant who had occasionally worked with Seekay, not because he liked him but because the weird detective's abilities impressed him.

"Grann? Seekay. I have a favor to ask of you. On the Vinton affair."

There was a crackle of language, simmering at last into angry coherency. "You were there? Were you the guy who knocked out two of the boys and—"

"You know I'm never lawless, Grann," Seekay interrupted. There was a smile in his voice if not on his lips. "About this favor: if you'll be still till I ask it, and then grant it to me, I think I can produce your killer."

"All right," Grann said guardedly. "What is it?"

"I want you to say that Vinton isn't dead," Seekay told him. "I want you to say that he was hurt, but not badly, that he soon recovered, and that he's insisting on still making the trip by plane to Florida tonight. You understand?"

"You don't want somebody to know he's dead, huh? But who do I give this phony dope to—the news hawks?"

"No," said Seekay. "Not the papers. Phone it to Vinton's secretary. Hines. Oh, yes, and tell Hines that Katherine Hart will go with Vinton. They will leave from my place, in a cab, at eleven o'clock for the airport."

CHAPTER THREE

THE OTHER MASKED MAN

AT ELEVEN o'clock that evening to the minute, Seekay and Marian heard a taxi pull up in front of Seekay's narrow, tall, secretive looking house. Seekay had phoned, in Vinton's name, for the cab to come and take him and "Katherine Hart" to the airport to catch the Florida plane.

"Ready?" said Seekay to Marian.

She nodded. Little chills were playing up and down her spine. In the dim light of Seekay's office, she seemed to be standing beside Robert Vinton. There was his face, detail for detail, under the grey felt hat Seekay wore. His body was that of Vinton—the tall detective could create an illusion of being smaller or larger than he actually was, by posture, walk and gesture, that was uncanny. The voice which had asked, "Ready?" was that of Vinton. Had not Marian seen Robert Vinton lying dead in his own library she'd have sworn that he stood here beside her.

The two started down the hall. Seekay had two bags with him, to carry out the pretense of a man on his way south. Marian wore Katherine Hart's clothes. They were a fair fit. She said, "What was the stuff in the little vial you took from the laboratory?"

"Distillation of *oenanthe crocata.*"

Marian opened the vestibule door for them both, as Seekay's hands were full. In the brighter light, at such close range, the death mask of Vinton which Seekay wore on his face gave her more than ever the shivery feeling that a corpse walked beside her. The very fact that its artificiality was slightly revealed, made the feeling stronger: it was the shocking artificiality that appears in all dead faces.

"Why are we doing this, Seekay?" she asked. "If you don't mind telling me—"

"I don't mind," said Seekay. "It's like this. Two men have been killed to prevent them from going to some part of Florida on some errand of Katherine Hart's. Murder was done to stop those trips. Perhaps, if we undertake the trip ourselves—at least ostensibly—the person who doesn't want the trip to be made will attempt to murder *us*. Then we may find out something."

They saw the taxi through the glass of Seekay's outer door. Seekay turned to Marian—and spoke through the lips that looked so horribly like a dead man's.

"I wanted you to go with me because it is necessary for our murderer to think he can get both 'Vinton' and Katherine Hart. It makes a better trap of it. But you needn't be the bait for that trap."

Marian squeezed Seekay's solid arm in one of the rare moments of demonstration she permitted herself.

"Where you go, I'll go," she said. "I'm sure you're ready to meet any danger. You always are."

"Some day the preparations will fail," said Seekay somberly. "One can't *always* guess future events correctly. This may be the one time…."

Marian smiled and opened the outer door.

"Keep your head down," Seekay said in a low tone. They crossed the sidewalk from door to cab. Marian got in. Seekay, standing under a streetlight, told the driver to take them to the airport. For an instant his face was clearly revealed under the light. Then he too got in, and the cab started off.

MARIAN HAD a feeling that was becoming familiar to her as she continued to work for Seekay. A sensation of cold at the pit of her stomach, a tendency to laugh abruptly, and a bit hysterically, a clamminess of the palms of her hands.

The symptoms, in a word, of deadly danger looming near and plainly sensed.

And surely that feeling was justified now. Some one had murdered two men, in some dread fashion that she still could not figure out. Now that mysterious some one had supposedly been informed that the second victim was not a victim after all, and was being invited to try his murderous work again—on Seekay and herself.

The cab hummed south along the wide boulevard, then turned west on a smaller street.

Seekay had his right sleeve rolled up and was doing something to his arm. Marian couldn't see what, in the dimness of the cab.

"What—" she began.

Seekay's barely perceptible jerk of the head forward toward the driver, stopped her. The driver, Seekay intimated, might not be wholly beyond suspicion.

"What time is it?" she changed her intended words.

"Ten after eleven," Seekay said, in Vinton's voice.

Marian thought she saw the driver stiffen a little at the sound of the voice, but could not be sure. However, she was sure a moment later that she did see him stiffen—at something else.

The slight angle of his head indicated that he had glanced at his rearview mirror for an instant. Carefully, she turned and peered out the back window, head to one side so that the move would not be too obvious to any one behind. She was glad she had taken the precaution, because there *was* some one behind. A car back there, with small cowl lights glowing, was steadily keeping about a block behind them.

Seekay stared at her through the eyeholes in Vinton's death mask, and she nodded. And then their own cab changed its course. It turned north and down a very dark street just beyond the warehouse section, which was utterly deserted.

Seekay leaned forward, and tapped the window between them and the driver.

"Why are you going up there?" he demanded pee-vishly, in Vinton's voice. "This isn't the way to the airport, my man. We'll be late for the Florida plane."

He stopped talking. The car behind was within a few yards of the cab's rear bumper, now. From an alley to the right came another car. It forced the cab to the curb; not that the cab took much forcing: the driver's willingness added another proof that he was in on the play.

Two men jumped from the car behind, and two more from the car at the side. They came forward and wrenched open the cab door. The leader was masked.

"My God—it *is* Vinton—" came the wavering voice of one of the four who hung back a little with his hat brim down and hiding his face.

"Shut up, you fool!" snapped the masked leader. He turned to the two in the cab. "Out of there, you."

"But—" Seekay began to protest.

The leader and another man swarmed into the cab from each side. Seekay put up just enough fight to be convinc-ing. Beside him, Marian fought with real terror, but her strength was inadequate and there was a hand over her mouth to keep her from screaming. In an instant the hand was jerked away and something else put over mouth and nostrils.

She tried again and again to scream, and could not. The sick-sweet smell of ether clogged her lungs. The world began to whirl. She felt Seekay's struggles growing weaker beside her, and knew that he too was being anaesthetized.

This is the end, her mind told her hazily. Seekay was right. There is always a time when preparations fall short. And this was that time.

Her mind slipped into blackness....

THE SOUND came again…. Drip, drip, drip.

Somewhere some fluid was dropping slowly onto a substance that hollowly resounded to the light impact like a tiny drum. Drip, drip. It sounded like blood; and at its insistence, Seekay finally opened his eyes. He stared around him with bewilderment showing through the eyeholes of the death mask. The bewilderment quickly hardened to tense concentration as a voice sounded.

"Coming around, eh? About time."

Seekay stared harder. He was in a cellar of what seemed an abandoned tenement building. There was a rusted furnace close at hand, pipes rusted nearly through tracing along the low ceiling, water standing in puddles on the cracked cement. It was water dripping from one of the pipes onto a hollow spot in the floor that Seekay had heard. The scutter of a rat sounded now and then.

Light came from a candle stuck in the neck of a bottle. It illuminated three figures besides that of the bound detective, who half hung from an iron upright to which he was tied with heavy rope.

One of the figures was that of the masked man. The man wore a shabby overcoat, almost like that of a tramp. But the arrogant erectness of his carriage was not that of a tramp, and the voice coming from the thin lips under the mask was not that of one of the world's unfortunates. The coat was palpably part of a disguise.

Another of the three figures was that of a heavy-set youngish man with coarse brown hair and a scar alongside his twisted nose. An ex-pug, Seekay judged. A common or garden variety hood who was merely a tool of the masked man.

The third figure was that of Marian, and Seekay's eyes blazed dangerously as he stared at her.

Marian Ford was still unconscious from the effects of the ether. She too was bound and hung suspended by the wrists from an upright. But she had been the object of more attention than Seekay. She had been stripped, and hung there nude save for a flimsy silken wisp around her waist. The guttering candlelight shone without hindrance on the alabaster of her thighs and waist, on the snow white of her breasts.

The masked man had his back half-turned toward Seekay, busied with some task the detective could not see. He spoke over his shoulder.

"The great Seekay! Setting a trap—and getting caught in it himself!"

Seekay said nothing. He tried to see what the man was doing, and couldn't. Beside the man, on a dirty table, however, he caught sight of something that sent a queer deep glint into his black eyes. Just a glimpse of something with a curved glitter to it, lying on its side.

"You were clumsy, my friend," the masked man went on. "The mask of Vinton couldn't fool any one save at a distance."

Seekay spoke then, his voice calm.

"Its only intention was to fool from a distance. I was afraid you wouldn't try for me unless it was reported to you that apparently, impossibly, I really was Vinton. There was a man in front of my house to check on that, wasn't there?" But as Seekay spoke, his eyes dwelt speculatively, curiously, on the glittering curved surface of the thing lying on its side on the table.

The masked man nodded. "He thought he'd gone insane when he saw you from across the street where he was posted. I knew Vinton couldn't be alive, and yet I felt impelled to make sure—which is unfortunate for you and your pretty secretary. You'd have been alive tomorrow if you hadn't tried to trap me."

Seekay shrugged as much as his bonds would let him.

"I thought it worth a try to trap you. Success seemed likely. For you are not so smart, you know. Not smart when you sent a poisoned gunman to shoot me down so I couldn't be retained to guard the life of Vinton, since that instantly decided me to take a case I might otherwise have turned down. Not smart when you tried to hoodwink me into arresting Katherine Hart for your murders, since I have some slight ability to detect nuances of voices and I realized instantly that it was not Vinton who was calling the second time. No, you're not so smart as you thought you were, Doctor Frick."

THE MASKED man suddenly was as immobile as wood.

"What makes you think I am Frick?" he said at last.

"I know you are," said Seekay quietly. "Just as I knew Hines would phone you at once, on being told by the police of Vinton's continued life, to see if Vinton was physically able to stand the Florida trip after what had happened. So you can take off your mask any time."

A strangled oath came from the man's lips, but he whipped off the mask, glaring at Seekay.

"How did you know?" Doctor Frick snarled.

"Several details," Seekay replied, quite calmly. "In the first place, only an intimate of Vinton's could have known in advance that Vinton meant to retain me, and could have sent a murderer to kill me before I could take the job. In the second, Vinton's left sleeve was unbuttoned when I found him dead. Why? Because just before he died he had been continuing to undergo a physical examination 'to see if he was fit' to make a plane trip. Again, Hobart and Vinton were both killed by something constricting on their throats like a giant snake. What could it have been? Well, a sphygmanometer would have made that even, light bruise clear around their throats. The flattened rubber tube, designed to be inflated tightly around a man's arm to measure the arterial pulse, could strangle a man, if placed around his throat, more efficiently than any hangman's noose ever invented. Finally, the gangster who so foolishly walked into my office with a gun in his hand was poisoned by *oenanthe crocata*, a poison too subtle for any but a doctor to know. So an intimate and a doctor killed Vinton, and hence must be guilty of all the rest. You were inevitably the man."

Frick regained most of his coolness.

"Bah! You haven't proof of this that would stand up in court."

"Right," nodded Seekay. "Which is why I sought to trap you at the end."

"And got trapped yourself! Which makes *you* not so smart, Seekay. For your death now guarantees safety for me."

Seekay glanced at Marian. Her eyelids were fluttering, and her breathing was perceptibly louder. She was regaining consciousness. Seekay's eyes softened with pity for the facts that consciousness would presently force on her. Then he glanced at Frick who had resumed his unseen task. The man with the scar beside his twisted nose only stared at the three of them, and continued silent. He looked pale.

"Hobart and Vinton dead," Seekay mused. "The gangster, dead. Now Miss Ford and myself. Five people you will have on your soul. And all because you didn't want protectors of Katherine Hart to go to Florida for her. I can't believe anything lies in Florida worth that to any man."

"That's where you are wrong," said Frick. He stopped his unseen task, then, and turned. And in his hand Seekay saw a rusty iron hook, evidently picked up from refuse in the basement. Rusty? Yes—save for its point. Frick had been sharpening the point, rubbing against a bit of cement from the cracked floor. And now the point glittered needle sharp in the candlelight. Seekay's black eyes looked strained as he stared at it—and then at Marian Ford's white loveliness.

CHAPTER FOUR

JUSTICE OF SATAN

SO YOU can't believe that what lies in Florida isn't worth murdering for," said Frick, standing in front of Seekay and softly slapping the deadly hook into the palm of his left hand. "Katherine Hart could have told you differently.

"Katherine's an orphan, with her father's will naming Hobart and Vinton as executors. Among other things, her father left her several square miles of Florida land. Along the seacoast, but valueless because low and swampy. That is, it *was* valueless. Now, the government is going to build a super-highway right out along the sea, between her property and the ocean. It will make it invaluable. A development can go up there that will be as desirable as Coral Gables."

He stood slapping the curve of the crude hook into his palm, eyes glittering in a way that was not quite sane.

"The Florida property was more or less forgotten till this highway plan loomed up. Then, Katherine asked her uncle to investigate its location more thoroughly. She wasn't even sure it was that particular tract of land she owned. Hobart unfortunately died before he could go down. Vinton, on the way to make the same investigation, also unfortunately died. So now my path is clear. I can have one direction changed on the deed to the property, through a county clerk who likes money, and the Hart estate will own, not the valuable ocean frontage, but a swamp tract to the north which will lie outside the new road's breakwater instead of safely inside. I happen to own that particular tract myself."

"I see," said Seekay. Marian had opened her eyes at last, and was staring bewilderedly at them. But her eyes soon showed realization of the desperate plight they were in; showed realization and terror, but no hysteria. For the dozenth time Seekay had occasion to admire grimly the stuff of which his secretary was made.

"You have murdered, then," said Seekay, "to be able to switch worthless land for land worth millions, through a bribed land clerk."

Frick's mocking eyes went from Seekay to Marian.

"You want me to repeat myself now that your witness has regained consciousness," he sneered. "All right, I don't mind. Your accusation is correct. Did you hear, Miss Ford?"

"I heard," said Marian, and though the thin edge of horror underlay her voice, it was almost steady.

"Splendid," said Frick. He turned to the pallid roughneck with him. "Go out to the car, Shayne. I'll be with you in just a moment. Time to end all this."

"Oke," grunted the man. He left. And Seekay tensed a little. His bound arms started moving against his bonds. And Frick saw the move and laughed.

"That's one-inch rope, my friend. I hardly think you'll be able to break that. But in any event, it isn't necessary. You'll be free of it in a moment."

Seekay stared.

"Oh, yes," said Frick. "You can't he found here trussed up as you are. It would give the show away."

"The show?" said Seekay.

"Yes. An excellent show. With this hook, you are about to commit a most atrocious murder. You are to kill your charming companion in a way that only a sex-mad maniac would kill. At least that's what it will look like to the police when they find you. And they'll be even more sure you're a fiend when they see what lies under that mask on your face."

Seekay became very still.

"You—looked under my mask?" he said finally.

Frick's teeth were exposed in his tight grin. "I did. Most interesting."

"Well," said Seekay with a sigh. "After all, it doesn't matter. You'll be dead in a little while, I think."

FOR A moment Frick stared at the bound detective with something like alarm in his eyes. Seekay's tone sounded so positive. Then he laughed.

"You have nerve. But it won't stop the show, Seekay. Your secretary will be found, dead, rather badly treated with this hook. You will be found dead before her, with the hook in your hand, and with a beam from the ceiling crushing down on your skull. The beam will fall as a sort of justice of Satan on you for what you've done to the girl." Frick smirked at his own demoniac cleverness. "Back in your home, Katherine Hart will be found similarly dead. For I have decided it is necessary—*Oh, my God!*"

The last words came out in a scream of stunned horror as Frick stared with bulging eyes at Seekay. For Seekay, suddenly, incredibly, was bound no longer. His bonds seemed to have melted off his wrist, and, still bound at the ankles, he was falling outward toward the doctor.

The fall seemed slow. Actually it was a springing motion so swift that Frick hadn't a ghost of a chance of escaping the grimly clawing hands. His startled attempt to leap backward was arrested as though by a jerking cord, as Seekay's fingers closed on his throat.

He lashed out with the deadly hook, but Seekay twisted like an eel and avoided the frantic thrusts. He tried to scream again, to the man outside the building, for help. But the scream was only a strangled moan when it came from his distorted lips.

"So a little money in land is worth five murders, is it?" Seekay ground out, shaking the man like a rat. "And I am to be found dead and branded as a sex-mad killer, am I?"

Frick was not quite motionless, but Seekay suddenly dropped him, and looped his body back so he could reach his bound ankles, still tied to the upright. Down the right sleeve of his coat slid the thing that he had concealed in the cab in anticipation of bonds—a long, slim blade with a razor edge. He hacked at the rope around his ankles as Shayne leaped for him from the basement door. Shayne had been drawn by Frick's first scream as Seekay leaned toward him so unbelievably freed of his bonds.

Marian screamed as the gangster leaped. But Seekay was free by then. He only crouched under the charge, reached up and caught the man and brought him crashing to the floor. Shayne was a gorilla for strength. He arched his body and got to his feet again. He lashed out at the faceless detective in a kick that would have broken Seekay's ribs had it landed. But it did not land. Stepping back, Seekay caught the lashing heel and heaved up to help the leg on its flying journey.

Shayne cried out as his other leg was swept from under him by his own momentum. He crashed to the floor a second time, writhed, started to get up.

THERE WAS suddenly an amazing and dreadful transformation in him. His eyes, glaring at Seekay, grew glazed. His body began to jerk in convulsions, and a bloody froth suddenly bubbled from lips and nostrils. Precisely the kind of froth that had stained the face of the dead gangster back at Seekay's house.

"Good God," breathed Seekay.

It was over soon. The man's body kicked and jerked a little longer, and then was terribly still, with eyes locked open and staring and jaws strained apart.

Marian moistened her blanched lips and stared from the body to Seekay.

"Poisoned," breathed Seekay. "Poisoned—as that other was poisoned. Doomed immediately ahead of their task by Frick so that no living witness could remain to trap him."

Frick stirred on the floor. Seekay's eyes were like jet, harder, icier, than Marian had ever seen them. They seemed not like the eyes of a man at all, any more, but like the eyes of a mechanical thing. He scooped up water from a puddle in the dirty floor and dashed it in Frick's face. Coughing, Frick opened his eyes.

Seekay strode to Marian and loosened the rope that bound her. He put his suitcoat over her nakedness, and then turned as a strangling sound came from Frick.

The doctor was staring at the dead gangster—and laughing.

"*Oenanthe crocata,*" he wheezed. "As you said, a subtle poison, Seekay. It leaves no trace. You lose, my friend. Your only material witness to my guilt is dead. You can never prove your case against me now."

Seekay said nothing, only stared first at him and then at the curved glitter on the dusty table, with brilliant eyes.

"You say I murdered four men. Try to prove it! You will find that not one tangible bit of evidence is in existence to betray me in a law court. You may say I wanted to trade swamp land for land worth millions. Try to prove it! The deal hasn't yet been made, so that nothing exists on paper. You may say I actually confessed to murder. But it is only your word against mine. You have stopped me from gaining the Florida property, but I'll never go to the chair."

Seekay only stared at him, eyes like living jet.

"Well?" said Frick, wheezing laughter coming from the throat that had felt the bite of Seekay's iron fingers. "Why don't you gloat over me? You trapped me. Why don't you call the police?"

"I'm not going to gloat over you," said Seekay.

"That is discreet," wheezed Frick. "For you know it would be premature, don't you?" He felt of his throat. "You, with your cleverness will see that I have been cleverer still, won't you?"

"I think you could be proved guilty in a court of law, in spite of what you think," said Seekay. "But I don't believe you will ever face a jury."

Frick stared at him with his eyes suddenly narrowing. There was something odd in the faceless detective's voice.

"Now what do you mean by that?" the doctor snapped.

Seekay nodded toward the rickety old table, toward the curved, metallic glitter.

"I recognize my flask," he said. "You got that from my hip pocket, I believe."

"Yes," said Frick. "Nice of you to carry my favorite brand of liquor, Seekay. I enjoyed it thoroughly...."

His voice trailed off.

"Damn you," he said, after a moment. "Why are you looking at me like that?"

Seekay said, voice organ-deep: "A moment ago you spoke of a curious kind of justice. The justice of Satan, I think you phrased it. It begins to look as though you—who are so clever that the law can't touch you—have received Satan's justice."

"I—I don't understand—" But in the depths of Frick's eyes a look of dawning horror showed that he *did* understand.

"The liquor in that flask," said Seekay, "your favorite brand—came from a bottle in the pocket of the dead gunman you sent to kill me. The gunman who died of poison."

"Oh my God," wheezed Frick. "That liquor? Oh, my God!"

"I was going to turn it in to the police laboratory for analysis," said Seekay. "Apparently the analysis isn't necessary—now. *Oenanthe crocata.* As you said, a subtle poison leaving no damning chemical trace."

Frick lunged suddenly for the door. He never made it. Just inside, he fell to the floor. His body began to jerk. A trace of bloody foam came to his lips.

Seekay picked up his flask and put it in his pocket. Frick began to scream. It was horrible—a wild, brainless shriek that kept on and on. And to its hideous echoes, Seekay half led and half carried Marian out to the street. You could hardly hear the screaming there.

WIDOW OF THE TALKING HEAD

WHEN SPORTSMAN PILOT PALMER RICHARDS CRASHED IN THE JUNGLES, HIS MILLION-DOLLAR ESTATE HUNG FIRE, UNTIL FOUR TORTURED, ESCAPED CONVICTS BROUGHT INDISPUTABLE PROOF OF HIS DEATH TO MRS. RICHARDS—HER HUSBAND'S HEAD!... BUT SEEKAY, BIZARRE, FACELESS INVESTIGATOR HAD HIS OWN IDEAS ABOUT THE WEIRD CASE, THOUGH DEATH MUST STRIKE FOUR TIMES TO PROVE HIM RIGHT!

CHAPTER ONE
THE THING IN THE BOX

T**HE BIG** coupe stopped at the curb on the quiet Chicago back-street. Out of it stepped a singularly beautiful girl, tall and lithe, with deep blue eyes and tawny hair. A man followed her from the driver's side of the car. Tall as she was, he loomed a full six inches over her; and the breadth of his shoulders dwarfed her.

He joined her at the curb, and then it could be seen that there was something odd about this man so smartly clad in brown tweeds. Very swiftly, in the clear October morning air, the oddity defined itself.

It was his face. The eyes alone were alive, black and glittering, like living jet. The rest of the face was dead. His was not a face at all. It was a painted mask. For this was Seekay, bizarre detective, who had no face as far as the world knew.

"This is the address given over the phone?" Seekay asked Marian Ford, his secretary and able assistant.

The girl nodded, staring at the painted mask of a face, wondering as all the world wondered what lay behind that false artistry. The two started toward the iron-grilled entrance of the house.

The place before which they had stopped—a tall narrow house sandwiched in between two exclusive apartment

buildings, looked like a bank vault. And the bank symbol was appropriate enough. The house belonged to Palmer Richards, millionaire sportsman and playboy. That same Richards who not quite a year ago had crashed a plane over the Brazilian jungles. That same Richards whom rumor would not allow to die; who was reported time and again to have been seen in the jungles by adventurers. Now it was said that he was held captive by a savage tribe; now to be living a hermit's life alone; now to be imprisoned in an obscure Brazilian jail, by authorities who refused to believe in his identity. Dead, yet obstinately not dead, Richards was to the world at large.

There stood Seekay—unharmed—his masked face relentlessly cold.

Marian suddenly laid her lovely hand on Seekay's powerful forearm.

"Look!"

She did not point. Only by the inclination of her sea-blue eyes did she indicate what Seekay was to look at. His jet black eyes followed hers.

He saw a face at a third floor window of the square, stone house. It was a girl's face, wildly lovely, with silky hair stringing around it; a face somehow out of a nightmare, with great dark eyes glaring in haunted, maniac fashion. Then, abruptly, the face was withdrawn and Marian Ford and Seekay stared at each other.

"Come," said Seekay, going on toward the door.

He pushed the bell. A discreet-looking butler opened the door. His eyes widened a bit at sight of Seekay's ghastly mask of a face, but the expression was instantly controlled.

"Tell Mrs. Richards that Mr. Seekay is here to see her," the faceless detective said quietly.

The butler nodded, bowed them to chairs in the wide front hail and padded noiselessly up an adjoining staircase.

From upstairs there was one sharp, short cry. It seemed human, yet you could not be sure. Seekay looked at Marian again, with the face of the girl at the window in mind, but said nothing. It was a curious house they'd come to; one to which few had been admitted since Palmer Richards left eleven months ago for the trip ending in the plane crash.

A woman came down the staircase. She was as tall as Marian Ford and almost as beautiful. But her hair was deep black as were her eyes; and there was none of Marian Ford's warmth about her. She looked like a cold black panther, in her dark hostess dress. But she was cordial enough.

"Won't you come in here, please?"

SHE LED the way toward a small den off the hall. As they entered, once again came that sharp wild cry from somewhere above. The stately tigress smiled thinly.

"It is one of my sister's bad days," she murmured. "She is…." She concluded by touching her forehead.

They sat down, with Mrs. Richards at the desk. There was a paper on it. Seekay saw something like a list of names on it, then saw they were all the same name. Mrs. Helen P. Richards, written over and over. She put it in the top desk drawer.

"You were told by your secretary why I called?" she said.

Seekay nodded, black eyes glittering through the eye-holes of his mask, while the painted lips smiled gently and unnaturally.

"You are expecting proof of your husband's death, Mrs. Richards. The bearer of the proof is a doubtful character. You wanted some one on hand to protect you—and to make sure the proof is genuine."

"That is right," Mrs. Richards replied, face almost as expressionless as a mask itself. "That is, the first part is right. I may need protection. As for the second part—no one on earth is in a better position to know if the proof is genuine than I myself."

Seekay stared at her. The room seemed suddenly very still.

"How is that, Mrs. Richards?" he said finally. "What is this proof?"

She looked first at him and then at Marian. Her red, too-thin lips jerked a little. Then she said: "The proof is—my husband's head."

A slight sound from Marian told of an exclamation checked. But there was no other indication of surprise or alarm from her. She had worked too long for Seekay to be too shocked, even by the most fantastic of things.

"Your husband's head?" the faceless detective repeated. "That should he proof enough of his death."

"Some such undeniable proof is needed," Mrs. Richards said evenly. "You know how it has been. Mr. Richards has an insurance policy for eight hundred thousand dollars, and an annuity policy reverting to me of another hundred thousand. Almost a million dollars. But the insurance companies won't pay it over because it isn't legally proved that Palmer died in that plane crash. Every time a claim is pushed, some other silly explorer comes to light with a sworn statement that he saw my husband alive in the jungles. But if the insurance people see his head—they can no longer doubt."

"How is it that such... unusual... proof of death is coming to you?"

Mrs. Richards, as coolly as though talking of the fall weather, took a cigarette from a casket and offered the casket to Seekay and Marian, who refused. Seekay couldn't have smoked anyhow, through his mask.

"It seems that four men were in jail in an Amazonian town. They broke out and fled into deep jungle to escape. They were captured by savages who mutilated and tortured them terribly, but from whom they eventually managed to break free. Before they got away, they saw the dried head of a white man in the chief's hut. They had seen accounts of the plane crash of Palmer Richards, with pictures, and they recognized the head as his. At least that is what they swear. They had sense enough to realize the value of it, so when they escaped, they took it with them. One of the four will be here any minute now with the head."

"Escaped prisoners," nodded Seekay. "I can see why you needed some one around."

"Yes. Apparently the four are the most desperate kind of cutthroats."

"You are paying handsomely for this... proof?"

MRS. RICHARDS opened a desk drawer and took out five slim bundles of currency in her white, graceful hands that were so subtly like a panther's talons.

"Fifty thousand dollars, Mr. Seekay—"

The butler appeared at the door. He had kept his face fairly controlled at sight of Seekay's waxen countenance; but now it was agitated. Apparently he had just looked on something more disturbing than Seekay's facelessness.

"A man to see you, Mrs. Richards," he said, after moistening his lips. "He told me just to tell you he was from Brazil."

Mrs. Richards' white hands clenched, not in fear, but with a sort of animal wariness.

"Show him in."

Seekay studied her beautiful but glacial face. An odd woman. Any other, he would not have trusted to look upon so hideous a sight as her husband's severed head. Any other would be near to fainting. But Mrs. Palmer Richards, he was willing to wager, would exhibit no such signs of frailty.

A man crossed the threshold and stood a moment as the door behind him was closed by the butler. Then he walked toward where the three sat. Seekay's black eyes narrowed to jetty slits as he watched.

The man was of average height but more than average breadth. He walked with a limber, loose step hinting great physical power. And he kept his head down so that all they could see of his face was a glint of two pale eyes under the hat-brim.

"You are the man who got in touch with me yesterday?" Mrs. Richards said.

The man nodded. His left hand had been held a little behind him. He brought it forth now, and Marian bit her red lips. In that hand was a box about the size of those used to contain a standard-sized alarm clock. Three times too small for a human head. But its very smallness added horror.

"I have what you want," the man said, voice harsh and rusty as though long unused. "You have the money?"

Mrs. Richards pushed the piles of bills nearer to him on the desk top. The man set the box on his edge of the desk. It was tied with ordinary twine, which again somehow lent a note of horror to the thing. Instinctively you expected some container more elaborate than an ordinary cardboard box tied with ordinary cotton twine.

"Why is it that you don't take your hat off?" Mrs. Richards questioned sharply. "Why don't you show your face?"

"Lady," the man said, voice rusty and grating, "when you've been held for three months by jungle savages, and treated as jungle savages treat a prisoner they want to kill as slowly as possible, you don't show your face any more than you can help. Or any other part of you, as far as that goes."

His fingers worked with the knot on the twine.

"Nevertheless," said Mrs. Richards, "We want to see your face. There is room for plenty of dishonesty in a transaction like this. I can't allow you simply to walk in, take up fifty thousand dollars, and walk out again—without even having seen your face for future identification."

The man kept his head down. He had the knot half untied. "Better skip it, lady," he said. "It ain't that I'm afraid of being identified in the future that I keep my face to myself."

"I insist."

The man swore. "All right—you asked for it!"

He swept his hat off.

THIS TIME Marian's slight exclamation did sound out. And even Seekay's hands tightened. Mrs. Richards' healthy pallor became an unhealthy one, and her hand went toward her throat in the first gesture of agitation Seekay had seen her display.

The man had had reason to hide his face—or the remnant of a face left him by Brazilian head-hunters.

He had no eyelids. His reddened, suffering eyes, like bloodshot glass, dripped constant moisture and were periodically hidden by a hideous grimace that drew folds of flesh over them in a slight momentary relief. He had no lips, but the absence did not leave an unclosable hole in his face because he had no teeth either, and toothless jaws met closely enough for flesh to touch flesh where lips should be. His nose....

However, nothing would be served by listing the things that had been done to him in the jungle. It is enough to say that he had ample reason for keeping his hat on and holding the brim far down. Marian swallowed with difficulty—and wondered if Seekay's face, under the constant mask, were like that.

"You may—put your hat back on," Mrs. Richards faltered.

The man laughed, hard and sharp. Recovering his head, he turned to the little box again. He got the twine undone.

"This ain't pretty," he said. "You sure you want to see it, lady?"

"I must see it, of course," shrugged Mrs. Richards.

The man lifted the lid of the small box. Marian's hands were tight on the arms of her chair. Seekay's black eyes were riveted on the box.

"Here it is—red hair and all," the man said, callously thrusting his hand into the container.

Seekay jerked out an exclamation and rose with his gun in his hand with magic swiftness. The bark of the gun and the scream of the man sounded almost together. Almost.

But there was a tenth of a second delay between scream and gunshot. And in that fraction of time lay death.

The man staggered back from the desk, staring with terror at his hand, where two pin-pricks of blood appeared. On the desk writhed a small snake with coral-like markings. The snake was in two pieces, cut by Seekay's shot.

The box lay on its side, and it was empty. There had been no head in it—only the deadly coral-snake.

"Oh, my God!" screamed the man. And then he fell, and lay jerking and shuddering on the floor while the three watched in fascinated horror. In an incredibly short time the jerking and twitching stopped and the man lay still— and stark.

The telephone bell, a note eerie in its commonness, shrilled out....

CHAPTER TWO

SEEKAY'S DIAMOND

"LET ME," said Seekay, as Mrs. Richards reached for the phone.

He took it up. "Hello?"

"Mrs. Palmer Richards' house?" came a voice. Its rusty grating was like that in the voice of the man now dead on the floor.

"Yes," said Seekay, voice as calm as though nothing out of the ordinary had happened.

"You have just seen how a man dies when he thinks to cheat his pals," said the rusty, grating voice. "And you have also seen how an outsider, too, would die if he tried to play tricks on us. Does Mrs. Richards still want the proof of Palmer Richards' death?"

"Of course," said Seekay.

"Then she will be told tonight where to come and get it."

There was a click as the speaker hung up. And Seekay was halfway to the door before the phone had stopped swaying in its cradle. He raced down the hall and out the street door.

Whoever had called, must have been close to the house. Close enough to see the entrance of the man now dead. Otherwise he could not have timed his phone call so closely after tragedy had struck.

On the street, Seekay stared in both directions. A block and a half down was a drugstore. For speed, he jumped into his coupe and drove the short distance. But he did not get there in time to see see anybody on the sidewalk nearby who looked in the least suspicious. He went into the store.

A clerk behind the soda fountain approached him, staring curiously at his painted mask of a face. There were no customers in the place.

"A man used your phone booth a minute ago," Seekay said, making it a statement instead of a question.

The clerk nodded, watchful, hand under the counter. Evidently he distrusted as well as feared Seekay's mask.

"What did he look like?"

"I wouldn't know," said the clerk. "He kept his head down so his face couldn't be seen. He was a big guy, kind of poorly dressed. That's all I can tell you. He left in a hurry. I was scared of him—I don't exactly know why."

Seekay slowly left, and rolled the coupe back to Mrs. Richards' house. He had been a little too late to catch a murderer who had slipped a venomous snake into the box a double-crossing pal had carried to Mrs. Richards in an effort to get the fifty thousand reward all for himself.

Re-entering the house without ringing, simply letting himself in through a door he had left off the latch, he saw the butler struggling with a person at the head of the hall stairs. The person was the girl he had seen at the window—Mrs. Richards' sister.

"Let me go!" the girl was panting, hair stringing over her face. "Let me go—"

The butler saw Seekay standing by the outer door. With a powerful thrust of his arms, he got the girl back out of sight. There was the slam of a door, then the servant came downstairs. He nodded coolly to Seekay, and stepped to the door of the little den. At a motion of his head, Mrs. Richards came to him. Seekay heard a few words.

"…worse all the time. Institution…."

"We'll speak of that later," Mrs. Richards said. She walked to Seekay. In a moment Marian Ford came from the den and approached too.

"What do you advise me to do now?" Mrs. Richards asked Seekay.

The faceless detective turned his mask toward her, black eyes glittering, painted lips smiling gently, unnaturally.

"There is nothing to do but wait," he said. "When you get word where we're to go tonight for… your husband's head, let me know. I will be at my home."

"And the dead man in my house?"

"I will notify the police. There will be questions, but I think I can avoid anything more serious than that, and I think I can keep the reporters away for a time. Till I hear from you this evening…."

HE WENT out with Marian, and the two drove to his own tall, narrow house on the near North Side of Chicago. An odd house; in some ways as fantastic as its master.

In the tile-paved vestibule, Seekay stood facing the door, which was electrically operated.

"Open," he said.

The door, which would have withstood the assaults of crowbar and acetylene torch for many minutes, opened to the precise inflection of his voice. The two walked into a dim, cool hall.

"I'll see you in the laboratory at seven-thirty," Seekay said. "See that dinner is brought to my office at half-past six."

With darkness falling outside, Marian met Seekay in his laboratory at the appointed hour. The faceless detective had on the shield he wore in his own house, which was more comfortable than the exquisitely fashioned mask he wore outside. The shield was a plain celluloid sheet curving from below his chin to the line of his black hair.

Marian looked at him with a soft light in her blue eyes. She had passed some time ago from wondering what possibly grisly ruin lay under the mask, to a realization that she didn't really care. But Seekay seemed never to notice that look on her face which no other man had ever seen there before.

He stood a moment before a long table on which were many queer bits of laboratory apparatus. His eyes were wide in thought.

"You remember the circumstances of Mrs. Richards's marriage?" he asked at last.

Marian shook her head rather indifferently.

"I didn't, either," Seekay said. "I looked up as much as I could about it during the afternoon. It was a Cinderella tale, it seems. The woman, Helen Brant, was a Hollywood movie extra, with few friends and apparently without family. It wasn't even known that she had a sister—"

"She probably kept quiet about her sister because of her mental unbalance," Marian said.

"Perhaps," mused Seekay. "Anyhow, Palmer Richards married her and brought her here, where she didn't know a soul. And a week after the honeymoon he was off on one of his trips. So now he leaves a widow, who was only a bride of a month, to collect his fortune."

HE WAS moving now, as he spoke. He went to a tall cabinet in a corner and opened it. From it he took a package Marian recalled had been delivered late that afternoon. And this in turn yielded what looked like two pairs of extra heavy stockings. As she looked closer, she saw that they were fashioned of fine leather, feet and all, and were hip-length.

"Put these on over your bare legs," said Seekay, handing her the smaller pair of leather hose. "Then put your stockings on over them. The leather is flesh-colored, so it would not show too much."

Marian raised her dress; slipped off her stockings, and slid on the long leather hose. Then she put her stockings back on. The faceless detective already had his leather hose on under his tweed trousers. Marian got shoes from a locker large enough to accommodate her feet in the leather hose, and stood before him. Her legs, no less lovely in curve than before, were slightly less slim, that was all. She asked no questions; she never asked questions of Seekay.

The faceless detective, eyes vital and alive in the eye-holes of his pink celluloid shield, was studying a picture from a year-old newspaper. Marian looked at it with him. Pretty clear for a newspaper reproduction, it showed the face of a youngish man with thick hair and a hawk nose. The eyes were arrogant and under them were premature little bags of flesh. Underneath was the caption, "Palmer Richards off for the wilds by plane—"

Seekay put it in his pocket as the phone rang.

He got to it in two lithe strides. "Hello. Seekay speaking."

"This is Mrs. Richards," came the cold, musical voice he had heard that afternoon. "The men you know of have just been in contact with me."

"Their message?" said Seekay.

"We are to go to thirty-three forty-eight South Wilton Place. We are to go alone and tell no one."

"I'll be at your home in ten minutes," Seekay said.

He flipped through a city directory on the telephone stand.

"Thirty-three forty-eight South Wilton Place," he murmured. "Belonging to Mr. and Mrs. Hiram Stone.... They're the department store owners. I know the place. It's a thirty-room mansion in what is now the negro belt, unused for years, up for sale but with no bidders. So that's where our cutthroats from Brazil have gone to ground!"

He slipped a ring from his little finger and gave it to Marian. A big diamond glittered evilly in the setting with the move.

"You'll know what to do with this. Follow me in the roadster. If you hear a cry from me, let twenty minutes pass and then scream as loud as you can."

CHAPTER THREE
THE DEATH CHAMBER

IT WAS a chill, dark night, with spats of rain presaging an all-night drizzle. There was no one in sight on the sidewalk when Seekay stopped his coupe at the small side entrance of what had once been one of Chicago's greatest mansions.

Seekay, with Mrs. Richards dark and cold and lovely by his side, hurried across the walk to the side door of the disused old residence. Not a light showed behind that door, or anywhere else in the great pile of reddish stone. But as the two approached the portal, it swung open to receive them, with ancient hinges grating creakily.

Seekay paused on the threshold. He could see no one in the Stygian gloom of the small hall into which the side door opened. He could hear no sound. It was as though the door had opened by itself. He wondered if Marian had succeeded in following the coupe from Mrs. Richards' home to this South Side house. If so, she had done such an excellent job of it that he himself could not tell of her presence. Frequent glances into his rearview mirror had disclosed no following roadster.

"This—this is rather *frightening,*" whispered Mrs. Richards. "…frightening," came a whispering echo as her voice went through the empty old stonepile. "Should we—go in?"

"…*go in?*" came the whispered echo. She drew close to the faceless detective's shoulder.

"Of course," Seekay said. "…*course,*" came the echo.

He drew her forward. The door closed behind them like the jaw of some mysterious trap. Both turned. And now in the gloom Seekay could make out a moving form. It was that of a man, big head held low so that no pale blotch of his face could show.

"Upstairs," the man said. "…*stairs,*" came the echo.

Seekay walked toward a flight of steps more sensed than seen in the dimness. The man walked behind them. The echo of their footsteps doubled their presence.

They went up. "To the right," said the man behind them, at the top of the flight. There was no echo now. His voice was harsh, rusty. It was as though the man who had died in the Richards home that morning had come alive and was guiding them.

They turned right. Near the back of the great house, a door stood open. From this came the first light they had seen in the place, flickering, uncertain.

"Go in there."

Seekay turned in, with the woman's hand tense on his arm. Two men were in a room barren of all furnishings save a rough box on which was a bottle with a candle in it. The men had been sitting on the floor.

The two turned to stare grinningly at the faceless detective and Mrs. Richards. And as the man behind came up and joined his pals, he too stared—grinningly. None of them could stare any other way....

These three, in mutilation and horror, were identical with the man who had been murdered that morning. They too were without eyelids, lips, teeth. Their faces, too, were things out of a nightmare. Thought of the tortures to which the four from the Brazilian jungle must have been submitted before they escaped, was a thing to make an observer's blood run cold.

Seekay stared around. Opened cans, crusts of bread, milk bottles, told that the men had camped in here for some days. The place was like some unclean animals' den, just as the occupants' faces were like those of animals rather than of men.

THE MAN who had guided them up the stairs seemed to be the leader. He was the biggest of the three. He leered with a lipless mouth while his lidless eyes dripped moisture.

"So you're Mrs. Richards," he grated to the woman.

"I am," she said.

Seekay stared at her, impressed once again by her stony self control. Prepared for the appearance of these men by what she had seen in her own house that morning, she looked at them as composedly as though they'd been absolutely normal.

"So you're the one Pete thought he'd sell us out to," the man said "Well, Pete got his. I saw him start to sneak out with the head, so I put one of our little coral pets in the box where his hands'd touch it. You got the money for us that you were going to pay him?"

Mrs. Richards nodded and opened her purse. She showed the bundles of currency. Seekay could feel the three men crowd a bit closer, eyes avidly on the cash. His hand crept just a little way toward his gun.

"Okay," the big fellow said. "I'll get what you want."

He chuckled, and stepped to a door in the side wall. It opened on a room hidden in blackness. The candle glow did not penetrate in there. He went in, and was gone a moment. Seekay looked around some more. He saw dirty blankets over the windows, so the light couldn't be seen on the street, and a low tin tray in a corner like that from which small animals might feed. The thought was carried further by the fact that a little milk was in the bottom of the pan.

The man came back from the next room, kicking the door shut after him. He crossed the threshold in a hasty leap, and was very swift to shut the door. It was as though he were jumping out of the den of some dangerous beast.

His bloodshot, moisture-dripping eyes were on the woman's face. In his right hand he held a dull wooden box with a lid tightly closed over it.

"Here it is, lady," he grated. "The thing you want so badly. The head of your husband. There ain't enough money in the whole world to really pay us back for what we went through to get it. We could have got away from that headhuntin' outfit in Brazil twice as easy, if we hadn't made up our minds to go into the chief's hut and get this head before we left. It meant maybe getting caught again. And if you knew what those jungle devils can do to a prisoner without lettin' him die...."

The man shuddered, then shrugged.

"But we made it. We got the head and got away too."

Mrs. Richards stared at the man's horror of a face. She shivered a little. But the physical fear she palpably felt, was confined entirely to her shrinking body. Her eyes were as cool as black water; and so was her voice as she said:

"Let's see it. Naturally I'm handing this money over only after I see that the box has the proper contents."

"Yeah?" sneered the man.

"Yes. Once before, today, there was a box that was supposed to have Palmer Richards's head in it. And it contained something much different!"

"This has the head in it, all right." The man's fingers worked with the lid of the box, opened it. "And here you are."

In his gnarled, scarred hand, the man held a human head. He held it by the hair, which was sandy-red, so that it dangled down from it like a great bead from a mesh fastener.

THE HEAD, hardly bigger than a large orange, was perfect. It was that of a man with a large, hawk nose, and an arrogant mouth. There were even traces of Palmer Richards's baggy flesh prematurely under his eyes. Marvelous primitive skill had crushed the bone of the skull and removed it, and had hollowed the remaining features and filled them. Even Seekay, who had seen Richards only as a newspaper picture, *knew* this was the man's dried head.

The two other mutilated men from the jungle stared first at the ghastly thing and then at the woman. Seekay looked at it with eyes of living jet through the eyeholes of his mask, while his painted lips gently smiled. The woman stared as though at some quite ordinary object. Nerves of steel, she seemed to have.

"Well?" grated the man who held the severed, dried head.

Mrs. Richards nodded, with a sigh.

"It is his head," she said.

The man with the grisly thing in his hand stepped a little nearer her. Almost imperceptibly, the other two jungle derelicts moved nearer Seekay.

"You are sure, Mrs. Richards?" purred the leader of the three.

"I am absolutely certain. So will the insurance people be, when they see it—"

The man dropped the head, which rolled heedlessly into a corner, and sprang. His misshapen hands clamped over the woman's shoulders. As he moved, so did the other two. They got to Seekay with the swiftness of feral animals; and one pinioned his arms while the other jerked for the detective's gun.

It had all been so swiftly, that it seemed scarcely a full second was needed for the move. And then the two were prisoners.

"How dare you!" gasped the woman.

"What is the meaning of this—"

Her words were cut short by the cackling laugh of the leader.

"All we wanted to know, lady," he said, "was whether that is the head of Palmer Richards. We thought it was, but we couldn't be *sure*. And we just naturally had to be sure."

Helen Richards's lips parted and her smooth throat swelled.

The man raised a fist like a battered mallet.

"Yell just once," he said, "and I'll make your face look something like ours!"

The woman remained still. The man grinned liplessly and shook her in his hard grasp.

"You think we meant to be satisfied with a lousy fifty thousand dollars for a thing like this? Don't you think we know what it means to you? Damn near a million. And yet you meant to buy it for fifty grand."

The woman stared at him. She was scared now, but she still had a fair control over herself. The man continued.

"You should go to the jungles sometime, lady. You should see what we went through there. You should know what it meant to take that damned head. Do you know what they thought of it there?"

His dripping eyes glared into hers.

"The natives worshiped that head, like it was a god. Every day the tribe squatted before it, and rubbed their foreheads in the dirt. It was supposed to guide them. Yeah, they thought the thing could talk—they thought it *did* talk, to the chief, in the night, telling him what was best for them to do. Why, it was like takin' an idol out of an Indian temple, or like stealin' an altar from a church, or like carryin' off the gold crosses from a monastery to yank that head out and get away with it. Now we'll get a real payment for it. We'll take that insurance dough ourselves."

SEEKAY STRUGGLED in the grip of the other two. One of them raised his gun threateningly to bring it down on the detective's head. Seekay subsided.

"You're mad," whispered the woman. "How could you collect that money?"

The man's lipless grin broadened.

"Very simple, lady. You'll do it for us. You'll get it from the insurance companies, just like you planned, only you'll turn it over to us after you get it."

"You wouldn't dare—"

"You don't know what we've already dared. It'll be like this: I'll go back to your house with you. We'll get in without even your servants seeing me. I'll stay out of sight till you give the servants their discharge, and after that just you and me will stay in the place like a couple of turtle-doves. But only for a couple days. It won't take long. You'll have the insurance boys out and you'll show 'em that head, and you'll get your dough. Fast. And I'll be right near you, in another room, with a gun on your pretty back through a crack in a door. When the insurance checks are cashed, I'll go. *Now* do you understand?"

"You'd never get away with it," panted the woman.

"We'll see."

Mrs. Richards glanced at Seekay, held immobile between the two hard-muscled men, with only his jet black eyes moving.

"How about him?" she said.

The leader laughed. It was a dreadful sound, coming from his lipless mouth. He jerked his head toward the closed door leading into the adjoining room.

"That's simple, too, lady. You saw the snake that came from the box this morning in your house? Well, there are more of those little coral darlings around. They're in that room. Nine of 'em. We brought them up to sell to zoos, but we found a better use for 'em. Your friend with the mask will go in that room. And speaking of the mask, I think I'll take that myself. It's a damn smart thing—I could go around like a human being again, with that over my face."

"You'll throw—that man—into a room with nine deadly snakes running loose?"

"Yeah. And you too, beautiful, if you don't promise to do what we want."

The woman moistened her lips.

"I—all right. I'll do it."

"Okay." The leader released her and turned to the two who held Seekay.

"Right, boys. In with him."

A choked exclamation came from the lips under Seekay's gently smiling mask. He struggled again as the two dragged him toward the door.

One of them grasped the knob. He jerked the door open, and they catapulted Seekay into the dark room. Seekay's cry rang out then, with the swift slamming of the door on the crawling death shut in with him. He hammered at the door. The four in the room from which he had been thrown, could hear his feet wildly pounding the floor as he sought to kill the deadly coral lengths that he could not see.

"He'll get over that," said the leader. "He may get a couple. But nine? No chance."

The pounding on the floor and banging at the panels weakened. Seekay's cry came again, but not nearly so loud. There was a pause, a choking sound from the dark room, and then a crash.

CHAPTER FOUR
THE HEAD TALKS BACK!

THE THREE men ringed around the shrinking, frightened woman. "How many servants have you at the house?" snapped the leader.

"Two," the woman said. "A houseman and a maid and cook."

"Any one else?"

"No one else—"

"Damn you—talk straight! We've watched your house for days. There is some one else there. Some other woman."

The woman cowered from him.

"There's only my sister...."

"Well, that's some one else, isn't it? Your sister! The devil! How can we handle that?"

"She—she's not right mentally. We've been keeping her in a locked room. I hated to send her to an institution...."

You could see the vast relief of the three men.

"Oh! That's all right, then. I thought for a minute there was somebody else we'd have to kill.... We'll simply keep her as she has been kept. And you will fake sickness or something, so the insurance people will come to you instead of having you go to them. They'll do that, all right, for Mrs. Palmer Richards—"

In the unclean room, like a beasts' den, a low voice suddenly said, "She is not."

For a moment the silence following was like that preceding a thunder-clap. Then a choked cry came from the leader.

"Who said that?"

The three stared around like animals. One leaped to the hall door, ripped it open, and stared out.

"Nobody out there," he said, coming back.

"It *must* have been from the hall!" the leader jerked out. "There's no other place it could have come from. Scatter through the house. Look in every spot where—"

"The voice came from that corner," said the other of the three. He inclined his head. "It didn't come from the hall or anywhere else. It came from that corner."

"What the hell? There's nothing there but that head—"

"I know," said the man in a low, strangled tone. "But it's that corner the words came from."

The woman's panted exclamation was loud in the eerie silence. The leader cursed blusteringly.

"Are you trying to say—that the head talked? The head of a man dead a year?"

THE THREE stared at each other. Then the leader went to the head and bent low over it. By a freak of chance it had come to rest on the stump of the neck and was right side up. It seemed to stare back from closed, eyeless hollows over which the eyelashes of the lids were like thread in two roughly sewn, short seams.

"Those imps of the devil in the jungle swore the head talked—knew all things and had power from the sky. They swore it talked...."

"Ask it," said one of the other men hoarsely. The woman was swaying on her feet, hands pressed to her throat, staring at the ghastly head.

"Ask it what?" snapped the leader.

"Ask it about the woman. Ask if she *is* Mrs. Palmer Richards."

"Of all the crazy questions—"

"What else could it have meant? 'Mrs. Palmer Richards,' we said, and it said, 'she is not.' So, ask the thing if she's who she pretends to be."

"You fool! How could she be anything else—"

"Ask the head."

The leader stared at the head again. The candlelight sent flickering, crawling shadows over the slightly withered face.

"Is this woman Mrs. Palmer Richards?"

And the head said, *"No."*

"Blood of Satan!" whispered one of the men. "It does talk! The natives were right."

All three were shuddering like children now. The woman was glaring first at the head and then at them. "Oh, my God," she was gasping, over and over.

"This woman was not your wife while you were alive?"

"No."

The leader whirled on the woman with his horrible face even more contorted.

"You liar! You're not Richards's widow! Are you? Answer! *Are you?"*

The woman sank to her knees, as her legs refused to support her.

"No," she whispered.

The man towered over her, insane with rage.

"Talk! Do you hear?"

"Palmer Richards's real wife is in his home, now. She is the girl I've been passing off as my sister. I kept her locked up, made her sign things, practised imitating her signature so that soon I could lock her in an asylum and go on for the rest of my life taking her place. To keep any one from suspecting, I said that she was mildly insane, so it would account for anything she might say to visitors, or for attempts to escape."

"How could you take her place with people who knew her?"

"No one knew her. She hasn't a friend in Chicago. And she hadn't been here long enough for any of Palmer's friends to get to know her well. I used to double for her out in Hollywood, in long shots. I knew her there. When Richards crashed, I came secretly to Chicago, with this plan of getting the insurance money in mind, knowing I could do it, knowing I looked enough like her for casual acquaintances to be fooled into thinking I was the girl they might have met before Richards flew off to the jungle."

"Guess it's the truth this time, chief," one of the other men said, white face jerking. "So now what do we do? Our idea is out the window."

"Oh, no it's not!" said the leader. "We'll go right ahead. This jane, whoever she is, can collect just as she'd meant to before—and turn it over to us."

"It means we'll have to watch her closer," growled the other. "I wouldn't trust her with a broken beer bottle."

"Neither would I—"

ONCE MORE a voice, quiet and assured, sounded in the room. The three turned to stare at the head, and then as quickly whirled toward the door to the adjoining room. For it was not from the corner the unexpected voice had sounded this time, but from that door.

Seekay was crossing the threshold, walking easily, eyes alive in the deadness of his mask. He shut the door after him and stood there, with the candlelight playing eerily over him.

"Thank you for your frankness," he said to the cowering woman. "I suspected some such thing was the truth, the moment I saw the sheet on your desk where you'd been writing 'Helen P. Richards,' over and over again. That could only be the work of some one practising a signature. I thought my recent course of action might be the easiest way to hear of it from your own lips. And, it seems, it worked—"

The three men were out of their coma of surprise. They all leaped for the faceless detective.

"Kill him!"

The woman had her wits about her. Living as dangerously as she had for a year past, she was as cold and fast in brain as the men. She saw a chance to get away—and took it.

With one swift move she knocked the bottle holding the candle, off its box, plunging the room into darkness. Then she was at the door, and her scream came keening with despair as she found that door locked. The man who had looked into the hall had locked the door again when he closed it. There was a more desperate scream from her as the key fell from the lock under the frantic fumbling of her fingers, and slid with a clatter somewhere along the floor. She had gambled and lost.

She had lost more than she knew when she knocked out the light. For the room was darkened just as the leader was flying toward the spot where Seekay had stood. He found no body there and in the blackness fell against the door.

The door to the next room flew open.

"God!" he yelled. "The snakes!" They heard him slide on his shoulder far into the next room, and heard a scream like that of a mad animal.

"They've got me! One got me in the face!"

The other two men were at the hall door with the woman, trying as hard as she to get out of the place.

"Get out of here! They'll be crawling in here in a minute! Death for all of us!"

Seekay was feeling with his feet for the candle, not daring to put his bare hands down. One of the men screamed, "My ankle! *Help*—"

The other said no word. But when Seekay got the candle lit, he was writhing on the floor with his pal. And the woman stood paralyzed while a coral-snake crawled over her silken instep.

THERE WAS a pounding at the door. "Seekay!" came Marian Ford's wild voice. "Seekay—"

"All right," the detective called softly. "Be still out there. Just a minute."

He was moving slowly as he talked, toward the body of the man who had taken his gun. He got it. The snake was swaying uncertainly at the woman's feet, while four more struck venomously at Seekay's leather-protected legs.

He shot its head off with a bullet that gashed the woman's ankle. She fainted. Seekay stamped the life from the four serpents at his feet, shut the adjoining room door on whatever number of the reptiles might be left in there, and let Marian in.

She looked at the two men on the floor with great blue eyes, then caught at Seekay's arm. He put his other arm around her as she reeled unsteadily.

"You're all right?" she paid. "None—got you?"

"Not with the leather leggings," shrugged Seekay.

"I cut my way in after you through a downstairs window with your diamond, as you ordered," Marian said. "But before the twenty minutes were up and I was to scream and divert the men's attention downstairs—all this happened."

"I found a better diversion than your scream would have been," said Seekay. "A bit of ventriloquism, with Richard's head as a Charlie McCarthy. It was dark enough in the room, and the four in it were distracted enough, so that I could open that door a crack and throw my voice into the corner where the head is."

Marian sighed. She looked at the woman questioningly.

"Just fainted," said Seekay. "Not dying, as the men are."

"Then she'll live to get that insurance money—"

"She'll live to spend twenty years behind bars," Seekay interrupted harshly. "She isn't Mrs. Palmer Richards, as I suspected when she acted so inhumanly cold-blooded about a thing as fantastic as her husband's head!"

Marian gasped. "Why, then—That insane girl at her house!"

"Yes," nodded Seekay. "No more insane than you or I. The real Mrs. Richards, kept prisoner by that she-fiend. But she'll be released now, with a fortune to keep her contented."

Marian drew a deep breath. "So again you help out a fellow human from a desperate situation—just as you helped me when I first knew you. I wonder if you realize what a valuable person you are, Seekay?"

"Not valuable from a humanitarian standpoint," said the faceless detective. "Just trying to turn a wasted life into a fairly useful one, that's all."

He picked up the unconscious woman and walked out, with Marian beside him. And she wondered what was the secret behind that amazing, inexplicable bitterness—and also the secret behind the mask. Wondered, and realized that she might never know....